MURDER
ON THE
RED RIVER

Also by Marcie R. Rendon

Girl Gone Missing

MURDER ON THE RED RIVER

MARCIE R. RENDON

First published by Cinco Puntos Press in 2017.
This edition first published in 2021 by
Soho Press, Inc.
227 W 17th Street
New York, NY 10011

Library of Congress Cataloging-in-Publication Data is available.

ISBN 978-1-64129-388-4
eISBN 978-1-64129-377-8

Interior design by Janine Agro

Printed in the United States of America
10 9 8 7 6 5 4 3 2 1

gigawabamin, Jim—
see you the next time,
the next time
and the next time around.

MURDER
ON THE
RED RIVER

FARGO, THE NORTH DAKOTA SIDE OF THE RED RIVER

Sun-drenched wheat fields. The refrain ran through Cash's mind as she pulled open the Casbah's screen door. She stood still. Momentarily blinded, she waited for her eyes to adjust to the darkened barroom. Outside, the sun rested on the western horizon. Inside the Casbah it was always night. The wooden screen door *thunked* shut behind her. The bar smells—stale beer, cigarette smoke, sawdust and billiard chalk—welcomed her to her evening home.

Sun-drenched wheat fields, healing rays of god's love wash gently over me. Cash didn't like the word god. Even in her own mind it was written in lowercased letters. What had *he* ever done for her? *Sun-drenched wheat fields, healing rays of sun's love* . . . nah, didn't work. *Healing rays of god's love*—now *that* worked.

Her mind was always composing songs or stories. The long days in the field gave her plenty of time to think of things to write. If she ever found the time to put words to paper, that would be a different story. Words in her head didn't pay the rent. Or buy a beer. Maybe with her next paycheck, she would get a guitar. She could sing in the cab of the truck and wouldn't need to write things down. Maybe.

Ole Johnson sat on a stool at the twelve-foot-long mahogany bar. The Hamm's Beer Bear danced on cool sparkling waters over his head. Ole slid fifty cents to his brother, Carl, seated at his right. They had a nightly bet on whether Cash's hair, which just grazed the bottom of her butt, would get caught in the screen door. On the nights when that happened, she would kick back at the door with her right foot and jerk her hair into the bar after her.

Tonight, her hair escaped the trap.

Like every evening since she first walked into the Casbah a year ago, Cash put a couple quarters on the pool table before going up to the bar and ordering two Budweisers.

Without a word exchanged, Shorty Nelson, the

Casbah's bartender, popped the top on a Bud and slid it across the wooden bar toward her. She rolled the cool, sweaty bottle across her forehead. A cold jolt shot through her skin to the bone of her skull. It reminded Cash of the ice cream headaches she used to get as a kid.

She took a drink and felt the coolness soothe her parched throat until the fizz hit her empty belly. *Ahhhh*. She picked up the other bottle and held it against her left collarbone as she walked to an empty booth by the pool tables, her leather cue stick case slung over her shoulder—one she had made sitting in the cab of a beet truck waiting to unload at Crystal Sugar a couple summers ago. It had leather fringe that swung with her walk.

She could smell wheat coming off her cotton blouse. She had changed clothes before coming to the Casbah, but she supposed even her Ranchero, which sat at the end of the field all day, smelled like wheat too. Her whole world was wheat and chaff and stubble and the drone of combines and Ford trucks with clutches that stretched her short frame to the max. Sometimes, if she was lucky, the truck would have a radio she could tune in to some country music.

Gol' dang, if ol' man Willie wasn't already passed

out in one of the booths. He was wearing field clothes. His stubby German mustache, cut in the same style as the salt and pepper bangs that hung over his forehead, drooped over slack lips. Cash fought off an involuntary shudder. The Hamm's Beer clock behind the bar said 9:35.

Willie must have left the fields early. That is, if he ever went to the fields anymore. Cash figured his son did all the farming for him these days. Old drunk. She couldn't help but glance to see if the front of his pants were still dry. They were. She shook off the shudder again. Pitiful ol' man. Every time she came into the Casbah, which was dang near every night, ol' Willie already had a jump on her.

She leaned against a booth to watch a couple farm boys shoot pool, playing at being hustlers. There were four quarters ahead of her. She had never left the Red River Valley, but she knew these two didn't know jack about hustling. Once, a couple of guys had come in on leave from working the Montana ranches. They wore big silver belt buckles and Stetson hats to match, putting the farmers' duckbills to shame. All the blond farm girls in the bar had been atwitter for the week those boys were in Fargo.

Those two knew how to hustle. Another guy, home

on leave from 'Nam, knew how to shoot pool too. But most nights, the only competition Cash faced was drunk luck.

"You up, Cash?" one of farm boys asked her. She nodded, took a quick drag of her cigarette and gulped more beer.

For the next two hours, against a background of quiet farm talk at the bar and the occasional canned laughter from the TV set on the back counter, all that was heard was the *click-clack* of billiard balls and the *clunk* as one sank into a pocket and rolled down to the front gate with another *clack-clunk* against balls already in place.

Cash held the table, drinking free the whole time. When she did lose that night, it was because Jim Jenson, a lanky farmer from Hendrum, came up behind her as she stood plotting the next run of five balls. He wrapped his arms around her waist and breathed into her ear. "Take me home, Cash."

CASH FIRST MET JIM AT a pool tournament over at the Flame, a few blocks from the Casbah. She was shooting in their monthly singles' tournament, women's division, when the barmaid pointed out the tall, skinny farm guy who had sent a Budweiser her way. After she sank the 8-ball in the game she was playing, he ambled over and asked if she would be his partner in the couples' tournament. Said his name was Jim and he liked the way she cut the last 8-ball into the corner pocket. He figured as partners they ought to have a chance at the tournament money. He wasn't that much older than Cash and he didn't seem to mind the fact that she wasn't blond and blue-eyed.

That night they placed third and took home fifty bucks each with the kitty and side bets. Standing outside in the parking lot, smoking a cigarette, he asked where she usually played. When she said the Casbah, he laughed and made some comment about the high-class part of town. She slowly looked up at the neon-lit stripper winding her leg around a pole that graced the doorway above the Flame. He chuckled again. Said he might drop by the Casbah and shoot a few. Keep in practice for next month's tourney. But now he had to get home to the wife and kids.

Cash didn't think any more about him until he showed up at the Casbah a couple weeks later, cue case in hand. He became a regular there and they became partners at the Flame tournaments. The pool, the beer, the winning—one thing led to another. Right back to Cash's apartment, in fact, where Cash had asked, "What about your wife and kids?" and Jim had answered, "Don't worry about it." So she didn't.

She had a lifetime of not worrying about it.

TONIGHT HIS BREATH MOVED HER neckline hairs, goose bumps popped up along her arms. She shook him off, bent over the table and made a five-ball run. She missed her last pocket call. The guy she was playing hooted, "I knew I'd beat you, girl. Your lucky streak is at an end."

He ran his last four balls but couldn't sink the 8-ball in the side pocket. Cash missed her shot.

He missed his.

Only Carl and Ole saw Cash's slight shrug to Jim, a shrug asking, "What you want me to do?"

Jim wrapped his arm around her waist and nuzzled her neck again. She brushed him off and bent over the table, shot the 8-ball straight into her pocket, followed immediately by the cue ball.

"Buy me a Hamm's, girl," her opponent crowed. "Rack 'em up."

Cash broke down her cue instead, went to the bar, bought her opponent a Hamm's and finished her Bud.

Jim wrapped his arm around her and started walking toward the exit. She tapped Carl and Ole on the shoulder on their way out. "Drinking free again, huh?" said Carl.

"Look," said Ole, pointing at the TV with his bottle. "More of our boys are dead."

Jim and Cash stopped to look at the grainy black-and-white images of Hueys landing in rice paddies. The newscaster finished up with the Vietnam body count for the day, then images switched to the local news. Cash couldn't hear the announcer as a loud *whoop* surrounded the pool table. By the time the noise died down, the newscaster was heading into the nightly weather.

Cash leaned into Jim to get him moving back out the door. The night had cooled down. Crickets chirped. Male frogs down by the Red River, which ran through town just a few blocks over, were croaking in hopes of attracting female frogs.

Cash and Jim walked the two blocks to her apartment over the Maytag Appliance store. A makeshift set of wooden stairs crisscrossed the alley side of the building up to the second story. The wooden door opened into a grimy kitchen. A stove plate rested on a cracked linoleum counter. Dirty dishes filled the sink.

Moths and mosquitoes batted against the screens of the open windows. Dust-covered jeans were thrown over the back of a wooden chair.

Cash opened the round-top refrigerator and grabbed two longneck Budweisers from the top shelf. She pushed the door shut with her hip and walked into the double-purpose living room that served as her bedroom as well.

She sat on the edge of the bed and took a drink before kicking off her shoes into the corner of the room. Another sip before she stood up, unzipped her jeans and stepped out of them, leaving them in a heap at the end of the bed. She walked around to the other end of the bed and sat cross-legged, pillow across her lap, back against the metal headboard, before taking another drink.

Jim undressed down to his white underwear and crawled into bed between the rumpled sheets. He put an arm around her waist and tried to pull her down to him. She said, "Lemmee finish this."

After the last swig, she set the bottle on the floor and lay full length into him.

Fifteen minutes later, she pulled her tangled hair out from under his back, pushed against his chest and brought herself to a seated position. "Time for you to leave, Farmer Jim." She lit a cigarette. "Your wife and kids are waiting."

Jim groaned and covered his head with a pillow. Cash pulled the pillow off and said, "Come on, get up. I gotta work early." She went into the kitchen and pulled out another Bud. She took a long gulp as she walked back to the bedroom. Half the beer was gone when she set it on the worn end table. She crawled into bed, pulling the covers off Jim and wrapping them around herself. She faced away from him, "Go on now. Lock the door on your way out." She finished her cigarette, swallowed the last of her beer and was out cold.

Jim rolled to a sitting position on the edge of the mattress, pulling his socks and jeans on, then fumbled in the dark for his shoes. As he buttoned his shirt, he leaned over Cash and kissed her forehead. She swatted, without waking, as if brushing off a mosquito.

He clicked the lock before pulling the door shut behind him.

MOORHEAD, THE MINNESOTA SIDE OF THE RED RIVER

Cash got up the next morning, a Friday, and walked to the Casbah to retrieve her Ranchero. She drove across the bridge to Moorhead before turning north into farm country on the Minnesota side of the river. Both small cities—Fargo and Moorhead—are married to the Red River, which meanders beyond the Canadian border. As Cash drove, the sun came up, warming the morning air, causing mist to rise from the trees lining the river.

Folks, Cash included, didn't think anything of putting on a hundred miles in a day's worth of driving. Everything here was *just around the corner*. But *just around the corner* could be thirty miles or more. If a stranger stopped and asked where the Wang farm was, chances are the answer would be similar: *Just a bit up the road*—meaning five or ten miles.

Farmers got up at 4:30 to eat breakfast before driving into the Fargo Implement shop to buy tractor parts, which opened at 7:30 A.M. They drove back to the farm, replaced the parts and spent until sundown in the field. Without cleaning up, many would make the three or four or ten miles into the nearest town for a beer before heading home to shower up, eat the wife's home-cooked meal, go to bed and start the day over again the next morning.

This time of the morning was Cash's favorite time to drive. The only other folks out were farmers and farm laborers like herself. She lifted four fingers off the steering wheel in a courtesy wave as she passed them.

She loved the vast expanse of farmland in either direction. Fields of wheat or oats stood waiting to be combined. Potatoes still in the ground. Hayfields plowed under, straight black furrows from one end of a field to another, the Red River tree line a green snake heading north. The leaves giving just a hint of fall colors.

She remembered someone telling her that the river was used to send furs north to Hudson Bay in Canada in the early 1800s. Once the area was open for homesteading, the plains on either side of the river filled with Scandinavian immigrants, felling trees and marveling at the rich topsoil. Some became the richest farmers in America, usually the ones who hired on folks like Cash. Others struggled, barely making ends meet with the harsh winters, springtime floods and short growing season.

The Red River Valley—or just the Valley as folks born and raised there called it—wasn't even a valley. Cash had learned in seventh-grade social studies class that the Valley really was an old glacial lake bed. All of this land was flat because some giant glacier had shaved it while moving north. Every year after that it flooded.

This year hadn't been too bad. Every spring the winter runoff of melted snow and ice from tributaries that fed the river would fill to overflowing. In the worst flood years, for as far as the eye could see in either direction, there would be a lake of muddy floodwater. Cash had spent many a spring helping sandbag the riverbank in Fargo or nearby farms in a fight with the rising waters. In those years, the Valley reverted to its original lake size. Floodwaters covered the area seventeen to twenty miles east, causing the river to disappear. The only way you could tell it was there was by the treetops meandering in the same direction Cash was now driving.

The social studies teacher, a farm kid who grew up and went to North Dakota State College and got a teaching degree because his dad wanted something better than farm life for his kids, proudly claimed the floods replenished the valley's two-foot thick, nutrient-rich topsoil.

Black gold, as the farmers called it. So while the growing season this far north was short—usually from May to August, with potato and beet harvest going into September and October—this part of the country, this country that Cash called her own, was known to the locals as the breadbasket of the world.

CASH HAD BEEN WORKING AS a farm laborer since she was eleven, when one of her foster mothers—one in a long line of foster mothers—decided she couldn't stand the sight of Cash. Something about Cash's dark hair and perpetually tanned skin next to the foster mother's blond daughter's peeling sunburn drove the woman crazy. She banished Cash to the fields to work with the men.

At eleven, Cash was barely four foot, nine inches and certainly less than a hundred pounds. A shave over five feet is where she stood now and more than a sack of potatoes, she thought. Back then she was smaller than the hay bales she was required to throw or the potato sacks she was told to fill. But she was quick and smart and what she lacked in physical strength, she made up for in sheer determination.

The men laughed at her size, admired her willpower and soon had her driving tractor and truck that had foot gears rigged with wooden two-by-fours so she could reach.

When the farm boys teased her about being a girl working with the men and asked why she was driving tractor instead of canning pickled beets, she would always reply, "I need the cash." Except the only cash she got was from her foster father when he hired her out to the neighboring farmers—he would only give her ten dollars of whatever they were paying. By the end of beet hauling season that first year, Renee Blackbear was forgotten and Cash was the girl-kid farm laborer all the men knew.

After a season in the fields, Cash decided there was no way she was going back to washing dishes, canning food and dusting ceramic trinkets from *the old world*. She started getting up a half hour early each morning and doing a routine of sit-ups, push-ups and isometric exercises she'd learned in sixth-grade gym class. All to build muscle strength. She sabotaged her housework by burning holes in sheets while ironing and over-seasoning whole kettles of stew meant to feed a household. While each insured a beating, it wasn't long before she was once again banished outdoors to work with the men.

NOW AT NINETEEN, CASH WORKED year-round as a farm laborer. At the end of each growing season, she drove grain truck from sunup to sundown.

This morning she drove north on Highway 75 on the Minnesota side of the river. She passed through the small sleeping towns of Kragnes, Georgetown, Perley and Hendrum one by one, nothing moving anywhere except for the occasional pickup truck.

When she got to Halstad, she turned toward the rising sun, away from the river. She parked at the Anderson farm, climbed into a Massey Ferguson grain truck and headed to the farm's north forty. She spent the day driving back and forth alongside the combine as it poured wheat into the bed of her truck. When it was full, she went back to the Anderson farm to unload. The truck creaked and groaned as she levered the bed to dump the grain. She stood guard, watching the grain flow with a thick, soft swoosh into the mouth of the auger, feeding it up into a steel bin.

At noon she ate lunch in the shade of the truck. She chased down a tuna sandwich with coffee from her red thermos, picking wheat chaff off the bread before taking a bite. For dessert, Anderson gave her a mason jar of homemade lemonade and a chocolate chip cookie his daughter had made for her 4-H project. Then it was back to work.

At twilight she got into her Ranchero and cruised through Halstad on her way south, revisiting the towns of the morning. Cars were parked headfirst in front of the liquor stores or bars in each town. Trucks were lined up at the grain elevators waiting to be weighed. Streetlights popped on.

Cash road on through Moorhead and crossed the river into Fargo. She ran up the stairs to her apartment, threw her work clothes into a pile on the floor and pulled on some cleaner clothes from the stack on the chair, heading back down the stairs and over to the Casbah.

The joint was full. Someone had stuffed quarters

into the jukebox and a couple of drunks were *Walking After Midnight* with Patsy Cline. Cash ordered a couple Buds and put her quarters on the table. She played till closing time, losing track of the number of games won and bottles drunk. At one point, some farmer dude grabbed her around the waist and slow danced while stroking her long hair, murmuring *ah baby* in her ear.

Jim showed up right at closing. Cash figured he had put the wife to bed, maybe taken her to a movie in Moorhead. She never asked about his wife, although rumor had it she had been head cheerleader back in high school. Cash also knew Jim hadn't been drafted because his older brothers were already serving. As the youngest brother, he had gotten a deferment to stay on the farm. Now Jim was at the Casbah for his Cash fix. Cash obliged and once again kicked him out in the wee hours of the morning.

SATURDAY CASH WOKE UP AT sunrise. Years of getting up at five to feed chickens, water dogs, milk cows and cook breakfasts was a habit more ingrained than the hangover from the alcohol she drank each night. Cash swung out of bed and put on the jeans she'd dropped on the floor the night before. She grabbed her shirt off the chair by the bedside and buttoned it up.

She needed coffee. She had a tin coffeepot like she had seen in the cowboy movies. She liked that she could dump in a handful of Folgers, put the whole thing on the hotplate, and by the time she'd tossed water over her face and brushed her teeth in the cracked porcelain sink in the small bathroom, the coffee would be boiling. She would shut the hotplate off so the grounds would settle and wait for it to cool a bit while she brushed out her hair.

Cash didn't pay much attention to her looks. Even now she shopped in the boys' section at JCPenney because boys' clothes were cheaper than girls' and the boys' jeans fit her skinny hips better than the ones in the women's or girls' department. However, her one vanity was her long, dark brown hair that hung low below her waist—all the guys in the bar raved about it. In one foster home, they had chopped it off—she had looked like a boy all that year. The humiliation of having her head shaved stuck with her to this day.

Cash turned on the radio and sat down at the small table in her makeshift kitchen to drink her morning coffee. The window overlooked the Northern Pacific Railroad tracks. If she leaned a little forward and to the left, she supposed she could catch a glimpse of the corner of the Casbah. But her attention was caught by the radio announcer talking about a body that was found in a stubble field thirty miles north of the FM area off Highway 75.

The broadcaster was saying Sheriff Wheaton had been sent out to check on a suspicious pile of rags in the middle of the field and found a body.

Cash jumped up, pulled on the cleanest dirty socks she could find, put on her tennis shoes and poured the remainder of the coffee into her Thermos. Within five minutes she was on Highway 75 headed north, back on the Minnesota side of the Red.

Thirty minutes later Cash leaned against her mud-spattered Ranchero and watched Wheaton talk with two men. Except for their black suits and Wheaton's sheriff's uniform, they could have been any three men discussing next year's corn crop, the price of wheat on the Minneapolis Grain Exchange or the odds that the Sox might take the World Series. All three stared down at the flattened stubble. A body lay there, his head facing toward the river, away from Cash.

Cash reached into the pocket of her jacket for a crumpled pack of Marlboros. She tapped one out and put it to her mouth, then fished in her jeans pocket for a book of matches. With a practiced left-hand move, she lit it one-handed by bending a match over the back of the matchbook. It was a trick she'd learned from one of the vets returning from Vietnam. In a drinking binge in a cornfield at the end of last summer, he had shown her the one-handed match trick. "You need it in the jungle," he said, "so you can keep your other hand on your rifle at all times. Of course, there are times when you are out on patrol and you just don't light up at all 'cause the tip of a lit cigarette lets the gooks know exactly where your head is."

Cash had practiced the one-handed trick over and over, suffering small black sulfur burns on her thumb before she got the hang of it. That soldier had re-upped as soon as he could. He had come into the Casbah for one last hangover before shipping out. Said he just couldn't make it out here in the real world. He was going back until the war was over or they shipped him home in a bag. Sometimes Cash thought about him and wondered where he was, other times she just didn't want to know.

She exhaled the smoke upward where it joined lazy fall clouds—fat like cotton candy—drifting slowly across the sunlit August sky.

The field where the men stood edged up to the Red

River tree line. Cash reckoned this close to the river it was probably feedlot corn a farmer grew, silage to feed his animals over the winter—not the cash crops of the larger acreage fields one or two miles away.

Cash put her left heel up on the Ranchero's front bumper and rested back on the hood, warmed by the late summer sun, wondering if the body in the field was cold or if the sun was warming him too. She couldn't tell much of what had happened to him. She assumed it wasn't a natural death or Wheaton wouldn't be here and neither would the two guys dressed in suits. Around here, men only wore suits for church or if they worked at the bank.

One of the suits bent over and lifted the dead man's left shoulder. It was then Cash got a look at the man's face—he was Indian. Wheaton glanced her way.

When she first pulled up, he had acknowledged Cash's presence with an imperceptible nod and a subtle hand gesture that she read as *Don't come closer*.

SHE AND WHEATON HAD KNOWN each other a long time. Back when she was three, her mother had rolled the car—with her three kids in it—in the big ditch north of town. All Cash remembered of that roller coaster ride was her brother and sister landing on top of her. Many times, come to think of it.

Wheaton had set Cash down on the long wooden bench in the waiting room of the jail while he went back out to the car to carry her mother in, even though her mother had walked out of the ditch perfectly coherent and rational when she explained to Wheaton that all she had done was swerve to miss a skunk. But then she must have passed out.

Wheaton laid her down in one of the cells without locking the barred door. Cash watched him walk farther back into the jail and return with a gray army blanket and a pillow. Talking more to himself than to the little girl on the wooden bench in his jail. In the dark of night, he muttered, "You'll have to sleep out here. I'm not putting no two-year-old in a cell, even though there's a bed in there. You don't need that memory haunting you. There, it's a little hard, but, hey, you have to use the bathroom or anything?"

Cash shook her head no. She thought it best she just stay put. She also didn't tell him she was three not two.

She could hear her mom breathing. She lay down on the bench. It was hard and the wool blanket was scratchy, but even at three, she knew it was best not to talk or complain.

Her brother and sister were at the county hospital, but the hospital wouldn't keep Cash because nothing appeared to be wrong with her. The nurses said the two older ones wouldn't be going to school the rest of the week and that the youngest was best kept with her mother. Wheaton had tried to argue with them. But maybe having to care for three children, two of them hurt—and a drunk mother—had made him give in to the hospital staff.

Cash had no memory of her first morning waking up in jail. No memory of what happened to her mom. Or her brother and sister, for that matter.

After that night came a succession of white foster homes, most of which she chose not to think too much about or remember. Once she learned to drive, she had been working any and all farm labor jobs anyone would hire her for.

And for whatever reason, she and Wheaton had developed a bond: he the county cop and she the county's lost child. He was the one who showed up for her track meets at school, the one who bought her a wool sweater each Christmas. She didn't have the heart to tell him the wool made her skin itch, probably because it reminded her of sleeping in his jailhouse.

He once brought a second-hand bike to one of the homes for her. She rode that bike until the tires were threadbare. When the county moved her, the family kept the bike, like they kept all good things. Anything new or worth something always stayed with the foster family. Cash left the homes with a paper bag or a small cardboard box of the shabby clothes she had arrived in. She missed that bike.

She didn't know why Wheaton looked out for her. Didn't ask. He didn't say. It worked for both of them.

WHEN SHE FIRST ARRIVED AT the field, there had been an exchange of words among the three men, who sent frequent scowls her way. Whatever Wheaton told them about Cash seemed to assuage their discomfort at having a fourth—actually fifth—person present at what was clearly a crime scene.

Their conversation finished, the two men shook Wheaton's hand and walked to their car, a black Olds. As they passed Cash, they looked at her but didn't speak. Cash took a drag of her cigarette and blew the smoke skyward.

Wheaton came over to the truck, kicked her front tire and said, "You might wanna put some air in here."

Cash nodded her head toward the car pulling away. "Who's that?"

"Federal folks, they said."

"What are they doing here?"

"The guy laying over there, I think, is from Red Lake. Federal jurisdiction."

"How'd he die?"

"Stabbed."

"Stabbed?"

"Yep. Looks like down over here. Come on." Wheaton walked back six yards on the gravel road. He knelt down, pointing with his right hand. "You can still see the blood. I think they must have stopped here to take a piss, and this guy got stabbed. The last time these ditches were mowed was some time last month. See how the grass is rolled down?"

"Maybe they just shoved him outta the car."

"Maybe."

"How'd he end up in the field then?"

"Guess they carried him."

"Why?"

"I don't know."

"Who is it?"

"Don't know for sure. No ID on him. He had a Red Lake baseball program folded up in his back pocket.

The feds said they were heading back north to talk to some folks up there. But them Red Lake folks keep to themselves. Doubt anyone will talk to them. The feds being white and all." Wheaton looked at her. "Not like they would talk to one of their own anyways."

Cash kicked a clump of dirt and smashed down another one, feeling the hard ball smush to silken silt. "Tell me more about this guy here. Can I go look?" she asked, already cutting down through the ditch and across the field to where the man lay. She walked between the rows of corn stubble, not wanting to get her ankles scratched up, her shoes making soft impressions in the dirt. When she got to the body, she saw the other footprints, including three sets that weren't Wheaton's cowboy boots or the suits' black dress shoes.

The marks were working men's shoes.

The dead man wore yellow leather work boots, blue jeans and a blue wool plaid shirt. She knelt down where she could see the cut that had gone through his shirt and into his chest. There were two stab wounds. One on the right, one on the left. "He was probably stabbed on the right from behind and then again there on the left. Whoever was doing it was aiming for the heart. Where's the knife?" asked Cash.

"That's what we wondered too. No knife that we've found. Other than that, not much to tell. Dead Indian. Looked like he was working. Didn't smell any alcohol. Fact is, if I had to say anything, I would say he must have been driving grain truck. You know how the chaff gets into all the cracks and creases of your clothes. Big guy too. Think whoever did this must have had to surprise him to get him down."

"I don't recognize him. But he does look like a Red Laker. Money?"

"None on him."

"Old man Fjelstad pays by check for folks working his fields." She paused. "Probably cause it's his bar in town that'll cash 'em."

Wheaton laughed. "Yeah, well," was all he said.

CASH SHIELDED HER EYES FROM the sun and looked up at Wheaton. He was a bit over six feet tall, sturdy, like maybe in his high school years he had played football but now, at the other end of his forties, he was just sturdy. Where the other Scandinavian farmers around here sported tan lines of white skin under their farmer hats or the back of their necks that wasn't covered by their shirt collars, Wheaton tended to overall tan.

When he took his sheriff's hat off to wipe his brow, the tan of his face almost matched the top half above his hat line and between his hairline.

He wasn't as dark as the man lying in the field, but he wasn't as white as the suits either. Cash often wondered about Wheaton and who his people were, but she had never worked up the courage to ask.

As long as she had known him, he had been the law. She had probably known him longer than she had known anyone in her life, but she really knew nothing about him. Only once had she been to his house. It was after a girls' out-of-town basketball game, and the school bus had arrived back late into town because of a snowstorm. She was living in a foster home outside of Ada, the county seat where Wheaton worked. The coach had let her into the school to call her foster dad. He was angry because the bus was late, had left instead of waiting for her and wasn't coming back into town again. Cash didn't know what to do. She couldn't walk home in a snowstorm, and the other kids' parents had already left.

Standing outside, shivering in the cold, Cash didn't know what to tell her coach, who was sitting in his car, engine running, ready to drive the couple of blocks to his own house. When Cash saw Wheaton drive by the school, she was scared enough to just once ask for help. She waved at him. He rolled down his car window. Through chattering teeth, she explained the situation. He opened the passenger door and said, "Get in."

Once at his house he had made her hot chocolate. He lit the pilot light of the gas oven, opened the door and told her to sit in front of it. The heat poured out and warmed her. It was a small house with almost nothing in it. No pictures on the walls. A small stack of plates in the cupboard that she saw when he opened the door to get her a cup for the hot chocolate. There was a well-worn couch in the living room and a small black-and-white TV set on an end table.

"You married?" she dared to ask.

"Nope. No time," he'd answered.

She took a long time to drink the milk, not wanting to leave the warmth. She finally set the empty cup down.

"Ready?" he asked.

"I guess."

On the drive out to the foster family, both of them were quiet. Wheaton said, "You go in and go to your room. I'm gonna have a short word with Mr. Hagen."

Cash did as she was told. For the rest of the winter, Mr. Hagen always picked her up on time. If Wheaton happened to drive by the school, Mr. Hagen would make a sloppy hand salute and say under his breath, "Yes sir, Chief." His wife stopped giving her desserts after supper. At the end of basketball season, the county social worker showed up and moved her to another farm in another township.

CASH SHOOK THE MEMORIES, STOOD and dusted the dirt off her hands and knee. She looked to the river and the tree line that snaked north. It was the land, this Valley, she felt the closest to. The land had never hurt her or left her. It fed and supported her in ways that humans never had. She heard the cottonwoods sing. Felt the rain coming before the clouds showed themselves. Smelled the snow before it arrived.

The town folks made fun of the farmers who would stand around in the fields, tamping dirt clods down with their work shoes, chewing a strand of straw or ditch grass, scanning the horizon. Town folks thought farmers were stupid because they didn't talk much. Cash knew—because she knew—each of them heard the land, felt the rhythm of the seasons. That tamping of dirt clods said how dry the fields were, told them when to pray in church for rain or for god to send the clouds away.

Standing in the field next to the man lying lifeless, she surveyed the land around her.

Her home reservation, White Earth, was forty miles to the east. She knew it was where her mother had been born and raised, except for a short stint in a federal boarding school. It was one of the things she seemed to remember someone telling her about her mom. Red Lake Reservation, where Wheaton seemed to think the man in the field was from, was about 135 miles northeast as the crows fly.

In 1968, the Valley was a draw for migrant farm-workers. In the spring, migrants from Mexico came north to hoe the weeds out of the beet fields. With wives and ten to twelve children per family, they spent the wet spring and muggy summers living in shacks not even the Indians would live in. Their language was fast. And often. A singsong of *eeee*'s wafted across the furrowed fields from early morning until late into the summer evenings as the smell of freshly made flour tortillas and magical spices drifted from their shacks.

Theirs was a musical language unlike the absence of language of the Swedes and Norwegians, many who still spoke with the heavy accent of their mother tongue, a deep brogue some were ashamed of and hoped their children would lose. They were a solid people who spoke mainly of rain and broken machinery or the cost of a bushel of wheat on the Grain Exchange. They listened to the farm market report each morning on the radio out of Minneapolis.

In the late summer and early fall, after the Mexican migrants had headed back south, another shift of farm migrants arrived. When they did speak, they spoke Ojibwe to each other in voices barely heard. A nod of the head could mean *Come here* or *Are you kidding me?* A hand gesture might say *Come closer* or *Don't you dare.* It was a body language so subtle it left some folks thinking the Indians could read each other's minds. Which wasn't unheard of either.

When talking to whites, they mostly didn't talk unless a yes or no was required. They had a different way of walking on the earth, even in the Red Wing lace-up boots they wore to keep the dirt and wheat chaff off their legs. They came to drive grain trucks up and down the wheat fields, to drive the beet trucks and then wait in line at the Crystal Sugarbeet plant just north of Fargo until the wee hours of the morning to unload before heading back to the fields. They came to load and stack hay bales and to put a hundred pounds of potatoes into gunnysacks.

Few came with family. Lone men and women off the neighboring reservations drifted into the small farm towns to work paycheck to paycheck. Some went back home on weekends, checks in their back pockets. Others drank away the money in the few bars that would serve Indians.

Cash vaguely remembered black-haired, dark-skinned aunties who spoke enough Spanish to get into the bars that refused to serve Indians but would serve Mexican migrants. The aunties would come stay for the season, sleeping on blankets rolled out on the floor of the tiny two-room house Cash's mom had lived in. When Cash thought about it today, she wasn't exactly sure who the aunties belonged to or how she belonged to them. Everyone older was an auntie or uncle, grandpa or grandma. Anyone close in age was designated cousin status. The workers who came to the Valley stuck together as family regardless of bloodline.

Cash never knew her father. She had a vague memory of her mom and the aunties talking about him coming back from the Korean War and buying the house in the Valley on his GI benefits. He had seen the world and wanted a life off the reservation. Her mom and aunties had laughed until tears ran their black mascara. Cash still didn't know what they found so funny about that. She remembered the aunties, their dark hair in pin curls, smoking filterless cigarettes, drinking boiled coffee, laughing about going into town, rolling the *eeee*'s off their tongues while they practiced saying town names like Hermosillo and Chihuahua as places to claim they were from if asked by the bartender.

There were other Indians who stayed in town. They roomed above the bars in makeshift hotels, where bar owners cashed the checks for room and drinks.

Cash looked at the man in the cornfield one last

time. He had probably roomed in town, although some of the richer farmers actually had bunkhouses for the late-season field workers.

She walked back to Wheaton's car with him. He had his hand on the door handle but she could tell he still had more to say to her.

He took his hat off and ran his hand over his buzz cut. He put his hat back on and raised an eyebrow. "What brought you out this way this morning? Thought you were working this week for old man Swenson?"

Cash shrugged. "You know how it is. Sometimes I just get a feeling and I follow it. I got up early and heard it on the news, so I drove out this way as fast as I could. When I passed Standard Oil in town"—she pointed with her lips to the east—"and looked over this way, I saw your cruiser and thought I'd come by and see what you were doing. You know." She shrugged again, her eyes asking if he understood. "Now I see you were probably wanting me to come this way anyways," she said. They both chuckled. It had happened many times before when Wheaton had thought about Cash and she had shown up moments later. Or the other way around.

"The thought did cross my mind," he said. "Listen,

I'm done here for the day. I imagine that if you pulled your truck up there in the Oye's driveway, up there by the migrant shacks, no one would bother you. Maybe stay around here for a while and see what you think. Those guys are headed up towards Red Lake. They won't be back for a while."

"You don't want to go up there yourself ?"

"Can't. Just like my badge doesn't do me any good over there on the North Dakota side," Wheaton said, pointing across the river, "us county law folks don't have any jurisdiction on Red Lake. Made it a law in '53. Red Lake's the only reservation in the state we can't go on anymore. I'm gonna drive into town and tell the county doc to come pick up this guy. Take him into the hospital and see if he can tell us anything else. You take it easy, Cash."

HE GOT INTO HIS CAR and made a U-turn on the gravel road, the stones rattling against each other. Cash watched the cloud of road dust billow behind him as he drove away. When the dust settled, she walked slowly back toward where the body lay. There wasn't much blood to see, just the flattened stubble, like a cow or deer had lain down in the field. She squatted and put her hand where the man's beating heart had been and felt the sadness from the earth crawl up her arm.

Chilled, with a shiver running up her left side, Cash stood and walked back to her Ranchero. She got in, slid the heat switch over to let warm air blow out the vents and then, to get some distance from the sadness emanating up from the earth where the man had died, she drove about 800 feet to the old driveway that led into the abandoned Oye's farmstead. Memory is what told her where the driveway was, as grass had grown up and over the gravel. Two strips of shorter grass indicated where cars and farm equipment had entered the farmstead years ago. The family had moved out to Montana. County gossip said that old man Oye had bought a ranch and had a thousand head of cattle.

Cash remembered back to when she was a child. Old man Oye would stop by to visit her mom, coming back from hunting trips out to Montana. Never any game in his truck but a pocketful of silver dollars that he would toss and spin in the air and hand out to whichever kids—white, Indian or Mexican—happened to be standing around waiting to be entertained. Older now, Cash figured the Montana trips were more about gambling than hunting.

When she was warm enough, she got out and

climbed into the back of her truck. She pulled an old quilt out from under a couple of two-by-fours, rolled up her jean jacket and laid down on her back. She put her hand over her eyes to shield them from the bright sun. Red sunlight filtered first through her fingers and then through the skin of her eyelids.

She could hear crickets and frogs down by the river. The leaves of the cottonwood trees lining the river bank created music in the wind that stilled her. Soon she was lost in time, her body floating up and out of the truck bed, following the trail of a soul gone northeast to say goodbye to loved ones. She saw a gravel road with a stand, almost like a food stand where one would sell berries, but this one had a basket of pinecones on it. Birchbark baskets were filled with pinecones. Children, five or six of them, crowded 'round the stand. The oldest was barely a teen. The youngest held on to the teen's scrawny hip. She looked around to memorize the place in her mind, searching for landmarks—the stand, the pine trees, a hunting trail heading north a bit down the road.

Was this the road where the children had come from? It ran east to west.

Just then Cash heard the dry crackle of leaves and smelled a faint odor of decay. It brought her back to her own body, lying in the truck bed of her Ranchero.

A deeper chill than even the one she had felt earlier caused her to sit up and put her jean jacket back on. She climbed out of the truck bed and reached into the open window for the pack of Marlboros sitting on the dash. She'd have to get another pack at Mickey's bar before driving back into Fargo. She lit the cigarette again with the left-handed move of the matchbook. It would be a few more hours before sunset, but this bend of the river seemed darker somehow and colder. She shivered.

CASH TOOK A LONG DRAG of her cigarette. She tried to remember the first time she had experienced leaving her body. In one foster home she'd been forced to sit for hours on a chair as punishment for one infraction or another. One day, in the middle of a daydream, she floated out of her body and into the yard where her foster mother was hanging men's work jeans on the line. Freaked out, she thudded back into her body on the chair, wondering what the heck had just happened.

That evening when the foster mother ordered her

off the chair and sent her out to bring in the laundry, Cash's heart jumped when she saw the clothesline hung with men's work jeans. She quickly swiped clothespins and jeans, threw them in the basket and hurried indoors.

One day that summer, at the Bookmobile, she read about a yogi who meditated and traveled out of his body. For the next six months, she checked out every book she could on meditation and practiced meditating when she was forced to sit on the chair. Needless to say, she got in a lot of practice. Meditation increased her intuition and also her ability to travel out of her body. While initially the experiences scared her, she practiced and got better at it until she had some measure of control over her travels.

Because she didn't have anyone else to ask, she decided to talk to Wheaton about her experiences. He was someone she trusted to not think she was too weird. He had looked at her over his coffee cup and said, "Yeah. I've heard some Indians can do that kinda stuff as well as India Indians. Just don't go floating off and not come back."

After a couple more sips of coffee, he had looked at her and said, "You have dreams too, I s'pose."

"Yeah, sometimes."

"Don't let them scare you. Just remember them. Someday you'll know why you have them."

Neither had ever talked about it again.

Half-finished with the cigarette, she climbed into the truck. Pushed in the clutch, shifted into reverse and backed out of the grassed-over driveway.

FARM WORK DIDN'T KNOW WEEKENDS. Laborers could get Sunday morning off to go to church, but it was Saturday and she was late for work. Svenson had five grown sons to help him out even if Cash never showed, but Cash was a woman of her word.

When she pulled into his driveway, Svenson's wife appeared at the farmhouse screen door, waved and hollered, "They're over at the old homestead, just drive on over," before letting the screen door slam behind her. Cash turned around and headed north another couple of miles to the old homestead. That was where Svenson's relatives from Norway had originally settled when the government was giving out 160 free acres to new immigrants. As each immigrant son came of age, they got married and started their own new homestead.

Cash pulled into the field crossing, parked and stood by her pickup waiting for the old man to come the length of the stubble wheat field. He was driving a Massey Ferguson tractor, pulling a plow behind it. The chug of the tractor's engine got louder as he approached, then silence filled the air when he shut it off at the end of the furrow. He climbed down. Cash could tell just from the way he moved that his arthritic knee was acting up.

"Sorry I'm late," she said.

Svenson wiped his brow with a red handkerchief he pulled from his back pocket. "If you can finish plowing this forty, I can run the wife into town. She wants to pick up some fixins for the church dinner on Sunday."

"Yep," said Cash, already climbing up on the tractor. Sven must have gotten to the field at sunup because he was more than half done. Cash plowed till about five, then drove the tractor and plow over to the field she knew Sven would plow next. She walked across the dirt furrows, climbed into her Ranchero and headed back to Fargo.

She took a quick bath and changed into clean clothes. She grabbed the thin quilt off her bed and a box of .22 shells from the top dresser drawer. Down at the Ranchero, she checked to make sure her .22 rifle was still behind the seat before heading back on the road. One of the things she had learned from all her out-of-body meditation practices was that sometimes she really did see things. Another thing she had learned over the years was the only person she could trust was herself—more often than not she chose to follow her quirky intuitions.

She drove north through Halstad and stopped in another smaller town to buy some cigarettes. She used the restroom of the town bar and continued north, cutting cross-country on gravel roads.

By the time she made it to some county junction, it was so dark and the township was so small that she missed the name as she entered the village. She cruised the main street, the only street, trying to decide between two bars, one on the south end of town, one on the north. The north-end one looked a little more rundown, probably a little more welcoming to a dark-haired female pool player. She pulled headfirst into a parking spot close to the one streetlight on the block, then reached into the glove box and pulled out a hairbrush, which she ran through her hair before braiding it down the middle of her back. Never knew what kind of trouble one could run into in these small-town bars in northern Minnesota. One braid was less of a handful to grab than a whole head of hair.

Cash reached behind the driver's seat and pulled

out her cue stick in its leather case. She hesitated a moment, then took the cue out of its case. She knew that white farm folks tended not to like anything too Indian up here, and she didn't want to risk damage to the one possession, next to the .22, she was attached to.

The place smelled like every other bar in the state. She scanned the place as she walked in. Noted the couple nuzzling in the back booth. The jukebox against the east wall. The mandatory town drunk on the end barstool, well into his nightly stupor. A couple of young farmer dudes shooting pool. They looked up at her, took in the cue stick and smirked at each other.

"Hey, baby, women's lib doesn't reach this far north," the one in a checkered shirt hollered.

His buddy, still wearing his manure-crusted work shoes, laughed and swigged a drink of his beer. "Wowee, we got a girlee here thinks she can shoot."

Cash walked up to the bar and ordered two Buds. The bartender asked to see her ID, which she pulled from the back pocket of her jeans. Cash looked him defiantly in the eyes as he scanned her identification. "You don't look a day over twelve, kid," is what he said, inspecting the front, back and edges of the ID. He still served her the beers. Cash walked over to the pool table, past two women sitting in another booth. Must be wives or girlfriends of the farmer boys. Cash put her beers on the ledge that lined the wall and her quarters up on the pool table. She perched on a red leather barstool to wait her turn and observed the ongoing game.

The guy with the crappy shoes wasn't half bad. Checkered Shirt couldn't bank for shit. She figured she would have to let them each win at least once, play for beers initially, then switch to cash in about an hour. By the time she would be done, she figured she would have to sleep in her Ranchero. Thank god, she was in the woods, the real woods, the pinewoods of northern Minnesota. Easy to hide a truck and a woman sleeping in it.

Checkered Shirt lost when he called the wrong pocket for the 8-ball.

Cash walked over to the table and slid her quarters in. The *clunk* of dropping balls was music to her ears. She put the rack on the table, flush with the green cushion, squatted, used two balls to a hand to fill the rack and positioned the balls just so. Stripe. Two solids. 8-ball between two stripes. Two solids, a stripe, a solid. Stripe, solid, stripe, solid, stripe completed the rack. She slid the rack back and forth positioning the lead stripe just so on the circle. The rack was tight. "Straight eight?"

Crusty Shoes answered, "We were playing last pocket, but I'll switch to straight eight for you, doll."

Doll, my ass. Cash chalked her cue while he postured for the break. She sipped her beer, resting her hip on the barstool. *Crack*. Balls scattered. Her opponent war-whooped as three balls dropped: two stripes and a solid. Being a gentleman he chose the solids and ran four. Cash made the fifteen and scratched trying for the eleven.

Cash overheard Checkered Shirt say to his girl, "She brought her own cue stick for looks. Can't shoot for shit." Cash let the farm boy win the game and put up another pair of quarters. She watched Checkered Shirt lose to Crusty Shoes. When their game was over, Cash smiled to herself, plugged in her quarters and asked her opponent if he wanted to play for beers.

"Sure," he said. Cash drank for free until closing time. Crusty Shoes was an easygoing loser. Checkered Shirt got more angry and foul-mouthed as the night wore on, complaining to his girl, wondering why the damn squaws don't stay on the reservation where they belong and how come drunken Indians were "takin' all my money, honey." Cash just played and drank.

When the bartender gave the last call, Cash scratched on the eight, shrugged, finished her beer and broke down her cue. As she walked by the boys' booth, Checkered Shirt's girlfriend slurred *bitch*. Cash, though tempted to finish something, steeled her resolve and left.

She lit up a Marlboro before turning the key in the ignition and backing out. She didn't feel drunk at all and wished she had bought a six-pack for the road. Too late now. As she headed out of town, she checked the rearview mirror more than once to make sure the boys and their girls hadn't decided to follow her. No headlights appeared. When the jack pines started to line the road on either side, she slowed and scanned for a turn-off road. It was too late to keep driving. She needed to sleep before hitting the reservation tomorrow.

About fifteen miles out of town, her headlights grazed the ruts of a logging road off to the right. She pulled in and drove about a quarter of a mile before backing her truck as close into the trees as she could get.

She stood in the dark and listened to the night sounds, her flashlight in one hand. In the far distance she could hear a car. A few minutes more, she saw the car continue north on the main road. She was in a good place. No one was going to come down this road tonight. She listened again before switching on the flashlight and scouring around in the truck bed of the Ranchero. After shaking the road dust off everything, she made a bed for herself with the quilt, covering herself with the wool blanket she had stashed there too. She went back into the cab and pulled her .22 from behind the seat, made sure it was loaded and went to sleep with it hidden under the quilt, her hand on the rifle butt.

THE SUN WOKE HER. THE fall morning air was crisp. She shoved the blankets back under the two-by-fours, unloaded the rifle, dropped the .22 bullets into her front pocket and put the rifle back in its place. She jumped in the cab and turned on the heat full blast. She lit up a cigarette and cranked the driver's window about three inches to let the smoke drift out. If she leaned forward on the steering wheel, she could see the occasional car drive by on the main road—farmers going into town for a needed part or to pick up feed. She finished her cigarette and crushed it out in the ashtray. *No point in starting a forest fire today*, she thought, shifting into first and pulling out into the overgrown ruts of the logging road. Her mouth tasted like stale beer and cigarettes. The thermos on the seat beside her had a mouthful of coffee left in it. Cold, but it covered the taste from the night before. Foolish to try the radio, nothing but static up here in the woods.

Cash smoked and drove. The weather was good. Sun was shining with the occasional thin white cloud. No cotton candy clouds today, just streaks of white. She thought about the stand she had seen along the road when she was lying down in her truck bed, the guy dead in the field with knife wounds in his back. Thought about the guys last night and the rugged comments they'd made about her.

There wasn't a name Cash hadn't been called: squaw, whore, stupid, heathen. She had heard them all. These days, she mostly just ignored irrelevant behavior. She shrugged and took another drag of her cigarette. Free beer and free games all night. What did she care?

Ahead she saw a sign that read: red lake reservation, no trespassers allowed. She laughed. These Red Lakers had all kinds of Indian Pride. Their reservation was the only closed reservation in the state. Meaning they didn't fall under state jurisdiction. Meaning they fell under federal jurisdiction. Which is what Wheaton meant when he said that as a county law man he didn't have any jurisdiction up this way. Which also explained the feds in the suits standing back there in a cornfield where a Red Laker's body had been found.

Cash finally reached the main road that halfway circled Red Lake, the lake itself.

She braked at the stop sign. Plain logic told her that if she turned east she would run into the town of Red Lake. If she followed that road farther north, it would take her to Ponemah, where they still practiced the old medicine. About the only people who took that road were folks who lived there.

Somehow that direction didn't feel right anyways. Cash turned left. She kept the truck in second gear and drove slowly, watching the sides of the road. The stand would be on the north side. She could see it in her mind's eye.

Here and there a crow flew. *There it was.* Gray weathered pine boards, probably from an old front porch, had been nailed together to create a three-by-four-foot table. The two legs on each end had branches from a birch tree nailed in an X to steady it. The ditch grass had been trampled down.

There was a driveway leading to the lake. Cash turned down it. Straight ahead, a fairly new boat sat at the lake's edge, with nets hanging on a makeshift rack close by.

Animal traps hung from another tree. And there, in the pines, was a rundown government HUD house. Weathered red paint. Unpainted steps led to the screen door that had seen too many kids and too many reservation dogs. At one time the window trim must have been painted white but was now a dirty gray. The picture window had a makeshift curtain, an Indian-print bedsheet. Even from the outside one could tell it was nailed back and that a safety pin held a corner up to let some light in.

The wornness of it reminded Cash of the house where she had spent the first three years of her life. Except her mom's house had been a two-room tarpaper shack—with no running water or indoor plumbing, which wasn't all that uncommon back then. Cash remembered visiting the white neighbor kids, who had outhouses too. But their houses were painted white. And they had a mom and a dad. Not just a mom living off the county, a mom who tended to drink a bit too much most weekends and ended up in the ditch more often than other mothers seemed to.

Cash remembered that after that roll in the ditch, the county social worker became the constant female adult in her life. She would pull into their driveway and load Cash into her big black Buick and drop her off at a different white farm home, where farmers' wives tended to harshness. Cash learned to duck her head out of a slap's way. She learned to take a beating stoically. She soon realized that behaviors that had made her mom throw her head back and laugh made these other women go red-faced and shame her into silence.

Cash became watchful. Wary. She didn't make too much noise or sudden moves. She did the dishes and swept the floors when told. She grew to know these women believed that cleanliness was next to godliness and that her permanently tanned skin was a mark of someone's sin.

She would go to bed each night in the stranger's house looking out the window at the stars, wishing for home. Back then, she didn't have a sense of time. Was she in one home a week? Two months? She never knew. She just knew the joy that filled her heart when the social worker pulled up and put her back into the thin, bare clothes she had arrived in.

In those first years, each time Cash had expected to be driven home. Back to her mom. It never happened. Cash searched each new school for her brother and sister. She didn't understand where her family had gone; why she never saw them and no one ever came to get her.

At their mom's, they always had something to eat, even if it wasn't the full spread the farmers' wives put out. Sometimes her mom didn't have the gas money to drive into town to get the water jugs filled and they would drink the rainwater from the rain barrels next to the house. They all slept curled in one big bed, kept warm by a kerosene stove in the winter months. There was always laughter. No swatting, no shaming. She and her brother climbed trees to the very top. She and her sister made mudpies and fed them to each other, their mom pouring a bucket of rainwater over them to wash them off.

Cash remembered other nights when Wheaton had stopped her mother. Told her she shouldn't be drinking and driving with kids in the car. Her mom would laugh and promise to get them home safely. He would always say to her as she turned the car back on, "Might be a good idea to stop drinking, you know." And her mother would laugh, say *sure* and wave goodbye.

Cash wished she could remember what happened the morning she woke up in jail. She had never gotten the courage to ask Wheaton.

With that thought, Cash threw the Ranchero into park and looked around the Red Lake yard, where she noticed various tire tracks. After surveying her surroundings, she directed her attention to the house and saw a shadow standing in what she assumed was the kitchen. She got out of the truck but quickly realized it was colder here by the lake than she had expected, so she reached back into the cab and put on her jean jacket and stuck the half-empty pack of Marlboros into the front left pocket. She walked up the worn steps and knocked on the door. A girl-child—about seven, black hair, with eyes just as black—cracked the door and looked up at her.

"Your ma home?"

The kid nodded.

"Can I talk to her?"

The girl shut the door and Cash waited, listening to the waves of the lake gently ease to shore. The woman who came to the door was a few inches taller than Cash. She was wearing a pair of black pants and a man's worn plaid work shirt. On her feet were scuffed penny loafers, no socks. Her hair was black, wavy, with strands that had escaped the rubber band holding it back. She couldn't help but notice her questioning eyes were as black as her daughter's.

Cash said, "Mind if I come in? I'm from down by Fargo, originally from White Earth, but been living and working in the Valley most of my life."

The woman said, "My husband is working down there, driving grain truck."

"Mind if I come in?" Cash asked again.

The woman opened the door and pointed with a tilt of her head to the kitchen table. Cash went over and sat down. In the center of the table were salt and pepper shakers, the glass kind you find in restaurants. A melamine plate with pale white commodity butter. A bowl with some sugar. An ashtray with a couple roll-your-own ends stubbed out in it.

Half the table was covered with more melamine plates. Each plate held beads of a different color: red, white, yellow, green. The front piece of a moccasin, half-beaded with a red flower, sat next to the plates of beads.

On the floor was a stack of three birchbark baskets, each with different size pinecones in it.

The woman placed a cup of hot coffee in front of Cash and motioned to the sugar bowl. She also set out a plate of smoked whitefish and a piece of frybread. She leaned against the kitchen counter and took a sip of coffee from a cup she had poured for herself.

"Thanks," said Cash. "I haven't eaten yet today."
I slept along the road last night. By the way, folks call
me Cash." She broke off some of the frybread. Without
a word, the woman handed her a knife. Cash used the
knife to spread some butter on the frybread.

While she was chewing, the woman spoke. "Did
you run into my husband down that way? Folks call
him Tony O. When he can, he plays baseball. Hits the
ball like that Cuban guy Tony Oliva that plays for
the Twins. You coming with news about him?"

She took another sip of her coffee without ever
meeting Cash's eyes. When she spoke again, there was
quietness in her voice that hadn't been there before.
"He's been working the fields down that way. He
should be home any day now."

"How long has he been gone?" Cash asked.

"Little less than a month."

"Well, I don't know anything for sure," Cash said,
picking bones out of a piece of whitefish.

"Sure you do," the woman said, sitting down at the
table and fingering the beads on the half-finished moccasin. "Shoulda been him pulling into the driveway,
not a stranger."

Cash looked at the woman, then back at the girl-
child hiding, peeking out from down the hallway.

Looked like there was a bathroom and probably three bedrooms that way. A tattered couch that had suffered one too many jumps from some child sat in the living room off the kitchen. A blue-and-white yarn god's eye hung above the couch.

Cash pulled the pack of Marlboros out of her pocket and offered the pack to the woman, who took one. Cash reached into her back jean pocket and pulled out a book of matches from the previous night's bar. Lit her own cigarette, then handed the book to the woman.

"You have other kids?" Cash asked.

The woman's eyes softened for a second and she answered, "Yes, five more. The bigger ones are out in the woods right now gathering pine cones."

"I saw the stand at the driveway. They sell to white folks?"

"Yeah, those white women paint 'em silver and gold for Christmas decorations. Buy 'em from the kids. The money helps out. Our baby's sleeping in the back bedroom. She's the reason Tony O went to drive truck this year. More mouths to feed. Most of the time we just get by with him fishing and trapping. Works on cars sometimes. But this year he decided to go to the Valley. You haven't said yet whether you seen him or not."

Cash took a drag of her cigarette. Blew the smoke out before answering. "I didn't meet him. And I'd hate to tell you something and be wrong."

The woman's eyes went back to wariness. "Tell me what you know. Long way to drive for not knowing me or him. I know you didn't just come for breakfast."

Cash looked at her and didn't know of any way to not say what she knew. She had never told anyone before that her husband was dead. She had never been the one to catch someone's first tears of rage or grief. She didn't know facts to share. She didn't even really know for sure the dead man was this woman's husband. And if it was her husband, she didn't know exactly how the woman's husband had come to be killed. What she knew was a knowing that had brought her to this woman's kitchen table. As she sat there and smoked and formed the words she would say, fear and tears built in the woman's eyes.

"Has he been hurt?" she asked. She stood up from the table and walked to the counter, to the sink and back to the table. "Is he in the county hospital? Is he hurt?"

"I don't know. There was a man killed," Cash said.

The woman flung her coffee cup into the sink. It shattered. Out of the corner of her eye, Cash saw the young girl skitter toward one of the back bedrooms.

"What the hell?" the woman yelled. Then she sat back down at the table. Put her head in her hands. Took a drag of her cigarette. Looked at Cash with eyes even blacker with rage, with fear. "What the hell you got to tell me?" The words breathed out with smoke.

"I don't know anything for sure. There was a man killed. The county sheriff, name's Wheaton, said there was no identification on him. There's some federal agents coming up this way today. I imagine they're over in Red Lake right now asking questions. They probably took some pictures and will be asking around trying to identify who died back there."

"So what are you doing here? How the hell did you get here? You don't even know it's him."

"No, I don't. Wheaton, the county sheriff, thought it might be a good thing if I drove up, tried to find out some things."

"You don't even know if it's my husband. Lots of men from here go down and work the fields."

"I know. I told you I don't know anything for sure. What I do know is that I dreamt that pinecone stand down at your driveway. Guess that's why I pulled in here."

"You dreamt that?"

"Yeah. Sorta. Maybe more like I went to the field where this guy died and saw the stand."

Tears ran down the woman's cheeks. "Saw it?" she asked. She fumbled for the cigarette in the ashtray only to realize all that was left was the butt. Cash took out another Marlboro, lit it and handed it to her before lighting one for herself.

"Yeah. I'm sorry. I could be wrong. I hope I'm wrong."

"You hope you're wrong." The woman snorted as she sat smoking, looking out the window toward the lake.

Cash heard the girl-child coming back down the hallway, stopping at the corner, not giving up her place where she could run back to safety if need be. Cash looked at her for a few seconds before a black Ford sedan pulled into the driveway. She and the woman watched the two men—the same two who had stood in the field back down in the valley by Red River—get out of the car. The car doors slamming silenced the woods and the lake.

The two men stared at Cash's truck. For a moment, Cash was worried they recognized her Ranchero from the field where Tony O's body had lain, but the men's attention quickly turned to the boat, then to the house.

She decided it might be better to be out of sight just in case. She heard a baby babbling and saw her opportunity. She stood up and said, "I'll go sit with the baby if you want." The woman nodded. In those seconds, the anger was gone. The fear was gone. The loss was gone. The woman's face had become a mirror of emptiness.

Cash got up and moved down the hallway, following the girl-child, who led her to the first doorway. Cash paused, looking in the room and seeing an Indian baby swing, gently moving above a double bed covered with a worn quilt.

There was a sharp rap at the screen door and Cash watched the girl-child run down the hallway to the door and crack it open the same six inches she had opened it for Cash. A deep voice said, "Is your mother home?" The little girl shut the door, looked at her mom and ran back toward Cash. They both went into the bedroom. The girl crawled up on the mattress and pushed the swing that was heavy with baby. Cash sat on the edge of the bed quietly, so as to overhear the conversation happening in the kitchen.

"Are you Josie Day Dodge?" was the first question asked by one of the men in the black suits. The woman must have nodded because the next question was, "We have a photograph here, not a pretty picture. But we need you to look at it." There was another long pause.

The baby stirred in the swing, made noises that threatened to turn into wails. The girl looked at Cash and tipped the swing a little so Cash could see the baby. Swaddled tight, arms straight down her sides. All Cash could see were two chubby cheeks, black eyes that must run in the family, and the porcupine-quill hairdo—two-inch-long black hair that stuck straight up. When the baby's eyes caught Cash's, there was a faint smile and a pleasant babbling sound. Cash leaned back and rolled the baby out of the swing into her arms, the movement causing the bed to creak.

One of the men out in the kitchen asked, "Someone else here?"

Josie Day Dodge—now Cash at least knew her name—answered in a voice tight with grief, "Just my cousin and the babies."

"Mind if we look?" Footsteps without an answer. Neither Cash nor the girl looked up at the man when he stood in the doorway. Cash ran her fingers through the baby's porcupine hair while the girl sat on her knees next to Cash, looking intently into the baby's eyes. Out of the corner of her eye, Cash saw black polished shoes—of nicer leather than the farmers around the Valley wore to church—and the black legs of creased suit pants. The shoes stood there a moment and then turned and walked back into the other room.

"Just a young girl and two little ones, one's just a baby," he said to his partner. Cash could tell from their voices they were still standing. *Dang, she could use a smoke.*

"So, Mrs. Day Dodge, you know this man?"

Josie must have nodded yes 'cause the next question was, "And he was your husband?" Cash could almost hear her nod yes.

"Do you have any idea who would have hurt him?"

"He just went down there to drive grain truck so we could have some money this winter. How'd he die?"

"Someone stabbed him. We aim to find out who. Who'd he go down there with?"

"No one. He hitched down that way from Bemidj-town a few weeks ago."

"Did he send you any money? Any letters?"

"No."

"All right, Mrs. Day Dodge. I think we should just head back into Bemidji, Carl. Maybe if we ask around in the bars over that way, we can get a better picture of who he went down there with."

"I told you he went by himself, hitched out of

Bemidj-." Cash could hear the silent rage in Josie's voice.

"Sure. Don't suppose you have a phone you'd be able to call us from if you remembered something or decided you wanted to talk to us?"

Cash brushed the baby's hair straight up and imagined the cold rage in the mother's eyes. She didn't hear Josie give a response but heard the screen door shut and the sound of shoes on the gravel, followed by two car doors closing and the engine starting.

Cash looked at the baby and into the other girl's eyes. They hadn't said a word to each other yet. They listened to Josie open and shut cabinet doors. Sounded like a glass and a heavier glass object being set hard on the counter. Cash heard liquid run. The girl looked at Cash, her eyes now sad. Cash put the baby back in the swing and stood. She glanced back at the girl to see if she was coming. The little girl just gently pushed the baby in the swing back and forth, the slump of her shoulders telling Cash what she would see when she walked out into the kitchen.

Josie sat at the table. A bottle of Jim Beam and a Kerr jelly jar half-filled with amber liquor sat in front of her.

Cash said, "Ah, man, don't do that."

"Go to hell," said Josie. "Just go to hell." She took a drink and shut her eyes as the liquid went down her throat.

"What about your kids?" asked Cash.

"What about 'em?"

"They lost their dad. Don't need to lose you too."

Josie took another drink. "Like I said, go to hell." At that point, she dropped her head on crossed arms on the table and broke into deep sobs. "What the hell am I going to do?" she asked. "We have seven kids. Seven."

Cash sat down on the chair where she had sat before and lit up a cigarette. Smoked through the sobs. Josie's shoulders shook. The girl peeked from around the corner of the hallway. Cash motioned for her to go back to the baby in the bedroom.

"Seven kids and each other, that's all we had. Just each other, that's all we had." More sobs. Cash stubbed out her cigarette and got up to pour herself some lukewarm coffee. Ate another chunk of smoked fish and frybread. Lit another cigarette. Josie lifted her head and motioned with her chin at Cash's cigarette.

Cash pulled one out and lit it for her, then put it into Josie's shaking hands. Her fingers were long, her nails neatly filed. Artist's hands, Cash thought. Or maybe just a mother's hands.

"Anyone you want me to go get?"

Josie shook her head. "The other kids'll be back before dark. I'll send the two older ones down the road to their auntie's." She took another drink of whiskey, emptying the jelly glass. "Haven't touched this stuff since the Fourth of July. He played baseball the whole weekend. Tournament over in Bemidj-."

More sobs.

"Hey, why'ntcha go. I gotta pull myself together here before the kids get home. Send them down to my sister's. She'll come down here with them. You go ahead and go. I don't know what the hell you're doing here anyways."

Cash stood, wondering what to say. Finally, she said, "The sheriff asked me to drive up. Thought I could break it easy to you. Give you a little heads up before those two got here. I'm driving back down today. Once I find out more about what happened, I'll come back up."

Tears streamed down Josie's face. Between hiccupped sobs, she said, "Can you make sure they send him up here all in one piece? None of that stuff they put in them white folks in place of blood. Send him back to me the way the Creator sent him here?"

"Sure. I'll tell Wheaton. I'll tell him that's what you

want. He's good people. He'll make sure the county listens."

Josie looked around, as if she was seeing her own kitchen for the first time, then poured more whiskey into the glass.

Cash said, "Whyn'tcha go a little easy on that until the kids get your sister over here?"

"Sure." She took another drink, wiped her nose and eyes on a corner of her shirt. "Sure."

Cash looked at Josie, then at the child who had come back to stand in the hallway. She walked over to her and knelt down. Held her at her shoulders, her skinny little girl shoulders, and looked in her deep black eyes. "My name is Cash. Can you say that?"

The little girl nodded.

"I want you to remember my name and tell your brother and sisters that Cash was here with your mom and will come back, okay? Your mama's having a hard time right now. It's going to be a hard time for a long time. You understand?"

Again the girl nodded.

"Cash. That's me. I gotta go. You go back in there with your baby and watch her, huh? Just go on now. Wait with the baby till your auntie gets here, okay?"

Once again the girl nodded and turned. Cash heard

the bedsprings creak as the girl-child crawled back up on the bed. Cash walked over to the kitchen table and dropped the cigarette pack on the table, figured there were about seven smokes left.

"I gotta go. Take it easy on that stuff. Your kids are gonna need you too, you know. And I'll tell Wheaton what you asked about his body not being messed with. Gigawabamin."

She left the house. Before she got to the Ranchero, she heard the jelly glass hit the wall inside the house and Josie wail with all her heart.

Cash got into her truck. It crossed her mind that she could go and try to find Josie's sister, but Cash knew that things sometimes just had to be the way they were. So when she got to the main road she turned right and fished around in the ashtray until she found a half-smoked butt. She pushed in the cigarette lighter and shifted into fourth.

When the lighter popped out, she held the bright orange coils to the cigarette, inhaled deeply, the smoke burning her lungs in a way a fresh cigarette didn't. She drove in silence, southwest, away from the reservation. She was tired but guessed it probably wasn't even noon yet. The federal guys would be over in Bemidji, getting silence from Indians on bar stools. She may as well head back to Wheaton and let him know that yes, the dead man was a Red Laker. To spare him some grief and worry, she probably wouldn't tell him that the man had left behind seven children. But she would do as she promised and tell him his wife wanted the body back whole, not cut up or embalmed like white folks did to their folks.

In the first town she came to, she stopped at a gas station, filled the truck and bought a pack of Marlboros. Once she hit the highway, she drove seventy, only letting up on the gas to coast through the small farming towns along the road. Traffic was nonexistent, just the occasional pickup truck headed into town.

CASH DROVE STRAIGHT TO THE Valley. Fields and electric poles whizzed by. Farmers were out plowing their fields, turning golden stubble down into the earth and turning up the rich soil that made the Red River Valley the breadbasket of the world. While wheat was still a favored crop, it was mostly potatoes and sugar beets feeding the world now. Some farmers were beginning to put in soybeans, hoping to get rich off them. Cash didn't know about that. Corn, wheat, oats, and, of course, the sugar beets and potatoes were what she had grown up knowing.

Cigarette after cigarette got her into Ada—the county seat—at about three in the afternoon. Wheaton's cop car sat outside the jail. A slight breeze furled and unfurled both the Minnesota and the American flags flying to the left of the jailhouse door. Every time Cash walked into the building, the smells, the granite floor underfoot, the clacking of the clerk typing, all sent her back to when she was three years old, being carried into the jail by Wheaton. Today was no different.

Even though she was nineteen, walking into the courthouse still made Cash nervous for other reasons. She had been here many times with the social worker, who was always so disappointed in Cash because none of the families she placed her with seemed to work out. The social worker carried a big black purse that matched her big black Buick, and Cash always felt like she, Cash, was just more dead weight in that big old purse.

She was supposed to have had a social worker until she was eighteen, but with only one to the county and Cash staying out of trouble, going to school and working full-time, the county had let her slide. By the time Cash was seventeen, she was living on her own in an apartment in Fargo. She'd been smoking since she was eleven, drinking too, but quiet-like, staying out of trouble.

Cash supposed Wheaton had something to do with the social worker leaving her alone. He was, in fact, the one who had gotten her an apartment in Fargo after he found her sitting in an August wheat field in the cab of a foster father's truck—long after the combines had quit for the night and all you could hear were crickets chirping, cars driving on gravel roads three miles away and lone dogs letting out a single bark. She had been chain-smoking and shivering, even though the night had been as hot at midnight as some summer days were at noon. Her face was tear-stained and she held a jackknife in her right hand.

Wheaton could see where she had thought about cutting the skin on her left wrist. He had taken the jack-knife first and then, without a word, had helped her out of the truck cab and into his car. That was her second and last night in jail. Once again he had made her a bed on the wooden bench in the waiting room. Cash had just laid down, faced the wall and gone to sleep.

In the morning, Wheaton gave her a mug of hot

coffee, black, and a jelly-filled Bismarck pastry. When she was done, he motioned with a slight tilt of his head for her to come outside with him. He had driven her into Fargo and talked the landlord into renting an apartment to his niece who needed a place 'cause his sister had died.

Cash shook away those memories and entered the county jail, walking straight to the sheriff 's door. She leaned against the door jamb. Wheaton had the phone to his ear and was sitting at his clerk's wooden desk. From there, he could see the two jail cells, both of which were empty this afternoon, and the familiar wooden bench. He motioned for Cash to have a chair next to the desk. Held up an open palm—*hang on a second*.

Cash picked up the morning *Fargo Forum* and scanned the headlines. More body counts out of Vietnam. She flipped to the funnies in the back.

From Wheaton's end of the phone conversation, Cash gathered that somewhere on the east side of the county someone had siphoned some gas from someone else's machinery fuel tank. Kids out driving the back-roads late at night tended to know which farmers kept gasoline on their farms to fill their machinery and which farmers didn't have German shepherds who barked.

Wheaton suggested to the farmer's wife that they put a padlock on the gas hose.

He hung up. "How you doin', Cash?"

"Been up to Red Lake and back."

"Oh yeah? Kinda figured you had headed up that way when you didn't come back into town. Find out anything?"

"His wife would like his body brought to her without anything done to it. No cutting out of anything or filling it with that fluid white folks put in their dead one's bodies."

"She say why?"

"Come on, Wheaton, you know as well as me those traditional folks back on the reservation don't like their dead bodies messed with. The whole body has to go on the journey. Up at Red Lake, most of the folks are still buried in those little houses they build above ground. I've only seen one or two places over at White Earth where they still do that. I told her you'd make sure he wasn't messed with."

"I'll go over to the county hospital in a bit. Make sure they leave him alone. What else did you find out?"

"Those fed guys got there about forty-five minutes after I did. Showed her a picture. It was her husband all right. Day Dodge. She said folks called him Tony O after the Twins player."

"Baseball player, huh?"

"Guess so."

"What'd the feds say?"

"Nothin' much. I stayed outta the way. They said they were going to go ask around in the bars in Bemidji to see who came down here with him, even though she had just told them he hitchhiked here by himself to make some money for the winter driving grain truck."

"Guess I can start asking around at the wheat farms then."

"Yeah."

"May as well get started. Not much going on here."

Wheaton stood up and went to the coat rack in the corner by the door. Put his official sheriff's hat on and his brown wool sheriff's jacket. From an inside pocket, he pulled out ten dollars in cash. He handed it to her.

"For gas and cigarette money. Anything else you see or hear you think I should know about? Those feds will spend about two days over in Bemidji, got a federal travel account. Will take them a while to decide they need to head back this way. I'd rather we figure this one out on our own. Haven't had a murder here since that migrant fight a couple years back. You see anything else?"

"Nah. I was just looking to see where he was from. I could go to the hospital with you, see the body."

"All righty. Let's go."

"I'll follow you. I want to head back to Fargo from there. Still in the clothes I wore yesterday."

They walked out together, got in their respective vehicles and drove the two blocks over to the county hospital.

There were four brick buildings in Ada—the bank, the jail, which was also the county courthouse, the school and the county hospital. Cash and Wheaton went around to the back, where the county's one ambulance was parked. They entered through a service door to a green corridor. The smell of alcohol and antiseptic hit their noses.

With each step, Wheaton's shoes made a sharp sound on the linoleum floor. Cash's tennis shoes were as muffled as the nurses silently padding through the hallway. One of them waved at Wheaton. In a town this small, everyone pretty much knew everyone else.

They turned a corner and went down marble stairs into the bowels of the hospital to the morgue. Wheaton pushed a button, which rang a doorbell behind a closed glass door. Cash could see sinks and metal tables on wheels.

Dr. Felix, the sole general practitioner for the county—and baby doctor and mortician—came walking up to them, slightly out of breath. He smelled of stale cigarette smoke and rubbing alcohol. "Sorry." He reached out to shake Wheaton's hand, ignoring Cash. He had nicotine stains between the pointer and middle finger of his right hand. Cash hoped he never had to operate on her.

"S'pose you're here to see the dead Indian? Come on in. The feds came by before they headed up north. I got the body back here in the freezer. Haven't heard anything from a family. Could be months before anyone even notices him missing. You know how these Indians are. Follow the checks and the bottle."

"Just show us the body," Wheaton interrupted him.

"Ah, sorry, Cash, didn't mean no offense to your people."

Like hell, thought Cash. In that moment she decided to die in another county. Any other county.

Doc Felix led them into the walk-in cooler. It reminded Cash of the egg cooler at the farm of one of the foster parents. That cooler was built into a corner of the chicken barn. The farmer stored the eggs there after Cash and the other foster kid woke up at five each morning to pack the 10,000 eggs that rolled in on conveyor belts. It was a dirty job. Next to pig shit, chicken shit must be the worst smell in the world. They would pack the eggs onto two-and-a-half-dozen flats, stack those flats twelve high, put twenty-four flats in one rectangle box and then put that box in the cooler.

Cash would be done by 6:30. She would try to wash the chicken-shit smell off her body before catching the bus the three miles into town for school. That was one in a long line of many foster homes she was more than happy to leave.

This cooler smelled like old people's flesh covered over with a healthy dose of antiseptic alcohol. Christ, she needed a cigarette. There were three bodies in the cooler, each on wheeled, metal tables. All were covered with sheets. The doc flipped back the sheet to look at the head of each body. "Grant Gunderson. Old Man Perley." He muttered before flipping back the sheet on a musty, dark-colored man.

"Here's your injun, Wheaton." Cash saw Wheaton's body stiffen, adding another half-inch to his six-foot frame.

"Show some respect for the dead, Doc. We know his

last name is Day Dodge. Goes by the nickname of Tony O. You could put that on the paperwork, all right?"

"Sure thing, Sheriff." Not the least bit contrite.

"You want to go put that on the paperwork." A statement from Wheaton, not really a question. Doc Felix left the room.

Wheaton and Cash stood looking at the body. Tony O was probably six feet. Black hair. Cash hoped to god Wheaton didn't decide to pull the sheet down farther. Being this close to death in a freezer was not her idea of a good time.

"What you think, Cash?"

"I think we need to get out of here."

"Yeah. Too cold and dead. They must have his clothes someplace, don't you think?"

"Yep. Let's go ask to see them."

Wheaton held the door open for Cash. The basement room now felt warm compared to the chill of it when they first came. She rubbed her forearms through her jean jacket, trying to wipe the cold away.

"I need to take a look at his belongings," Wheaton told the doctor.

He pushed away from his desk and walked over to a metal filing cabinet against a green-tiled wall. He opened the third drawer down and took hold of a paper bag, the red Piggly Wiggly logo on its side. He brought it back and set it on his desk.

"Not much in there," he said, picking through the stack of papers he had been working on. "Wrangler jeans, cotton work shirt—would guess from Sears Roebuck—wool socks, Red Wing work boots. Pack of Camels in the front shirt pocket. About thirty cents in change in the jean pocket. No billfold. And he was hanging loose."

A hint of a smile reached the doc's eyes and faded quickly when he met Wheaton's hard glare. "Just meant he wasn't wearing any underwear," he muttered, looking back down at the paperwork.

Cash reached over and opened the Piggly Wiggly bag. A draft of sorrow climbed up and swirled around her. In that moment she saw a group of Indian men laughing, wearing field clothes, leaning back on their heels. Two white men were standing off at a tree line. Cash just made out the shadow of a rifle before the paper bag was yanked from her hands and the doc said loudly, "Hey, come on now, I gotta keep this clean for the feds. Don't be con-tam-in-ate-ing the evidence!"

Cash turned and walked out. She heard Wheaton say to the doc, "Don't be cutting up Mr. Day Dodge. You leave his body intact, and none of that embalming fluid either. You hear me?" His voice turned as hard as Cash ever heard him talk. "Don't mess with this one, you hear me?"

Wheaton was behind her as they walked up the basement stairs, down the linoleum hallway and out into the fall sunlight.

Cash stopped by the Ranchero to light up. Wheaton stood in front of her. After a while, he said, "Sorry."

"Wasn't your fault." Cash breathed out smoke. "Just remember, if I die, for the love of god, don't bring me to this godforsaken place."

"Me either, all right?" Wheaton stuck out his hand for a deal shake. Cash took his big hand in both of hers and shook it. "When I opened that bag, I got the smell of death and two white guys watching a group of Indians. I gotta get back into Fargo. Need a change of clothes and to sleep in my own bed."

"You go do that. I'll talk to the farmers and see what I can find out. Figure that the day after tomorrow the feds will be back. Hope to know something before they do. You take care."

After Wheaton left, Cash rested against the car, enjoying the sun after the cold morgue. She finished her cigarette and smushed it out on the pavement, got into the Ranchero and headed south out of town, driving seventy all the way. Who was going to stop her? Wheaton? She laughed and turned on the country station. Waylon Jennings was wailing as she pulled into Fargo.

SHE PARKED IN FRONT OF her apartment and locked her truck. She climbed the stairs and was greeted by the stale smell of beer and cigarettes. She opened a couple windows to air out the place while she ran hot water into the clawfoot bathtub. She went into the bathroom, spun her hair up into a loop and hooked a pencil through it to hold it in place on top of her head. She undressed, dropping all her clothes in a heap on the floor.

She stood there naked for a minute, looking at the bath water that had already steamed over the mirror. There were parts of the bathroom floor where the linoleum had worn off or some previous tenant had ripped it up. When she walked across the floor, it creaked. There was a moment, every time, just before she stepped into the tub, that she wondered if the whole tub—filled with she didn't know how many gallons of water and her hundred and twenty pounds—might just sink through the floor, and there she would be, downstairs in the appliance store, a bare-assed Indian sitting in between washers, dryers and refrigerators.

She slid down into the steaming water, leaned back against the cold porcelain of the tub, enjoying the cold relief, which soon warmed to her skin. She tried to remember the name of the foster mother who had banished her from the bathroom in their house. Cash had tracked chickenshit on the living room carpet. Not only did she have to scrub the carpet, by hand, on her hands and knees, two times in fact, but the foster mother—screaming at the top of her lungs, swatting her all the while with a wet dishrag—told her she could never use the indoor bathroom again. For the rest of her stay there, Cash had washed up in the barn sink, the same sink she used to wash the chickenshit off the eggs each morning before packing them in cartons for delivery to the egg plant in Moorhead.

What the living room carpet had to do with the bathroom Cash had never figured out. But having her own bathtub, that no one could run her out of, was a privilege she cherished. She lay that way for about twenty minutes, replaying the events of the past few days behind her closed eyelids—standing out in the field where they had found Tony O, the pool game in Red Lake Falls, the visit to Josie's house, the feds, the morgue.

When the water turned lukewarm, she grabbed a washrag off the edge of the tub, lathered her body, rinsed and climbed out. She wrapped a towel around herself and scooped the pile of clothes up off the floor.

She walked out into the living room/bedroom and tossed the clothes in a basket that sat in the corner. Tomorrow she'd walk across the street and do her laundry, she thought. She dried herself off and crawled between the sheets of her bed. She reached over and grabbed her alarm clock off the top of the dresser and set it for half an hour. She lay down and fell right asleep.

When the alarm went off, she reached out and hit the off button. She stretched and yawned, pulling a couple long strands of hair off her lips and from across her cheeks. She jumped out of bed and rummaged in the dresser drawers for clean undies, socks and a bra. With her underclothes on, she looked over the pile of clean jeans and shirts that were hung semi-neatly across the back of the overstuffed chair that served as her closet.

She made herself a pot of coffee, thunking the two-day-old grounds into the wastebasket. For a moment she stood looking down at the cars moving through town, then opened the small fridge that stood in a corner of the room. Half a dozen eggs. Four slices of bread in a plastic bag. No butter. Someday she would have to go to the store. She took out an egg and two pieces of bread. The frying pan still had some butter in it from the last eggs she'd fried. This would work.

She made herself a semi-scrambled egg. When it was cooked, she put it between the two slices of bread with a dash of salt and plenty of pepper. By then her coffee was done and she sat down at the painted-white, chipped table and ate her dinner.

It was just a little before seven o'clock. Still light out. Plenty of time to drive down to Halstad and shoot a couple of games in Mickey's bar.

THERE WERE TWO BARS IN Halstad. Both sat right across from each other on Main Street, but only Mickey's had a pool table. Maybe she would go over to Arnie's first. Arnie thought his bar was high-class because he had a brand new jukebox and had cleared out the pool table to make room for a little dance floor. Cash supposed that on weekends the farmers brought their wives into town for a little flash. A respite from cooking three squares a day and breeding tow-headed farmhands. God save her from that life.

Cash laughed. She was the wrong color to live that dream. Arnie had rooms above his bar where maybe Tony O had stayed. All she had to do was have a couple drinks and she would be able to overhear any talk among the men. *A reconnaissance mission.*

As a little kid she had been her brother's scout in their many games of cowboys and Indians and remembered when he came home from school all excited about the new word he had learned—reconnaissance. A fancy word for scout or spy. He dressed Cash in black and sent her to spy on the neighbors down the road. The two of them crawled on their bellies through a corn field and swiped old man Johnson's food from his lunch bucket.

Later, in foster homes, she would do her own reconnaissance. She would sneak up under the kitchen window and listen to the social worker's conversations with the foster mother. She'd know ahead of time if she needed to start packing.

Cash brushed the crumbs off the table and into the sink thinking that—yep—after a trip to Arnie's, she could go to Mickey's and shoot a few games before heading back to Fargo.

Cash swung down Main Street and parked in front of the Casbah. She ran in and went straight to the cigarette machine at the back of the bar. The regulars were already there. She nodded at them as she walked back out. One of the pool players hollered after her, "You too good for us, Cash? See you got on clean jeans and shirt. Someone's getting lucky tonight, huh?"

"Yeah, you," Cash hollered back. "You get to keep the table till your beers kick in."

Laughter followed her out to the Ranchero. She headed north on Highway 75.

The song was back in her head. *Sun-drenched wheat fields. Healing rays of god's love.* She turned on the radio hoping to find a song to replace it, dialed in Oklahoma City. Pure country. Suicide music, as they called it in high school.

Back when she still went to high school in the country, she would ride around in an old Mercury with a bunch of boys. She forgot what year it was, but it had a back window that rolled down. It was the coolest ride in the county. It was Clyde Johnson's car. He worked summers building grain bins. Cash never knew if it was his idea or maybe his dad's. That family was always coming up with money-making business endeavors.

The grain bin business was Clyde's. The richest junior in the county. Even had his own work crew in the summertime. One of the first things he bought with his grain bin money was a fake ID. He would drive over to Ulen, where no one knew him and bring back a couple of cases of beer on the weekend.

None of the white girls were friends with Cash, so she drank with the boys, was thought of as one of them. Their church-going families, including the Catholics, understood their sons drinking with a squaw, but they better not date one. It would have disgraced their sorry families if one of them had dared to ask her to prom. But drinking? Why not? That's what Indians did, right?

Cash thought about all this as she drove north. There was about a mile of fields between the road and the river. Huge oak trees and cottonwoods followed the river down the Valley parallel to the road. The sun dropping to the west turned the field stubble to gold. Some wheat fields waved in the gentle breeze waiting for the swath of the combines. Some of the richer farmers were running three combines in tandem down a field with a string of five, six trucks waiting at the end to be loaded up with the grain. The color of the fields brought the song refrain back into her mind. *Healing rays of god's love.*

She turned the radio up full blast as Charlie Pride

found his way to San Antone. She lit a cigarette and cruised through Perley, then Hendrum. Just outside of Hendrum, she could see the Halstad water tower at the four-mile corner that would have taken her east, back to Ada. As a small child, riding around with her drunk mother, the water tower had been the thing to drive toward from either direction on the prairie. As long as she and her siblings could get her mother pointed in that direction, there was some hope of getting home.

Cash pulled into Halstad, stopping first at the liquor store to get a six-pack to keep the eggs and bread in her refrigerator company. The clerk pretended he didn't know her and asked to see her ID. "Can't be too sure," he said. "All these kids are getting fake ID's. Going over to Bismarck, some of them. I know you're living in Fargo," he said, admitting he actually knew who she was. Hell, everyone in the county knew who she was. The older ones had known her mother, the others had watched Cash make her way through just about every foster home in the county. Most of the men knew her by name and sight from field work.

Cash thanked him and carried the bag out, put it in the cab of the Ranchero and tossed her blanket on top of it. She drove past the Drive-Inn and headfirst into a parking spot by Mickey's. On Mickey's side of the street, grass grew up between the cracks of the sidewalk, a complete contrast to Arnie's side, where the grass was trimmed and the cars and trucks were newer. She locked up the truck but walked across the street to Arnie's. `

There were two concrete steps leading up into the bar. The new jukebox had Ray Price singing *For the Good Times* as a young farm couple waltzed on the makeshift dance floor. Cash stepped herself up on to a barstool. The bartender walked over, white bar rag tossed over his shoulder, and looked at her.

"Budweiser."

He put the bottle and a glass down on the bar. She motioned that she didn't need the glass and took a swig from the bottle. She turned around and faced the dance floor and booths against the east wall. There were six booths. Two of them had couples in them, sitting tight and cozy and drinking beer. One other booth had a pack of cigarettes, a pitcher of beer and a couple glasses on the table.

To her left were some young guys she didn't recognize. Probably from the Dakota side of the river, come over looking for a Minnesota girlfriend.

To her right was a cluster of older men, the wheat chaff still in the creases of their jeans and work boots.

They were talking. Cash caught a few phrases here and there. *Found him dead. Dead injun. Stabbed.*

"He was one of the drivers at Soren's last week. Quiet like all of them." Cash strained in to hear.

"Until they get a few drinks in them," another voice added. Out of the corner of her eye, she saw one of the men elbow the speaker and tilt his head in her direction, just slightly. They turned away and she couldn't hear them anymore. Cash sat and sipped and the lovers waltzed through Conway Twitty.

Into her second beer and another cigarette, the bar door opened and a young man walked in. He scanned the bar. When he saw Cash, he tried to appear casual as he walked up to the men at her right. They greeted him. When one of them called him John, he gave the guy a look that said *quiet* without a word spoken.

Cash kept sipping, smoking and watching the dancers, but her peripheral vision was sharp and set on all the nuances of the group of men to her right. The young guy said, "I gotta go. Naw, the other guys are busy."

Cash wondered who the other guys were, though she had a hunch she already knew. Maybe not their names, but she knew who they were. John walked out without ordering a beer. Clearly he had been scoping out the joint for someone else. Over the music on the jukebox, she heard an engine rev up and a vehicle drive west on Main.

She finished her beer and got down off the barstool. She waved a hand at the bartender and went outside. It was just getting dark. In the distance, she could hear kids hollering down at the school playground. Their mothers would be calling them home soon. Or, if they were well-behaved, they would head home on their own the darker it got.

Cash walked across the street to Mickey's. It was pointless to follow the young guy, even though she could still taste and see the dust lingering in the air telling her which direction he had driven. That handful of men at the south end of Arnie's bar knew she sometimes worked with Wheaton, so no doubt they were rubbernecking out the bar window behind the Grain Belt sign to see just where she was going. May as well shoot a couple games of pool. If the vehicle came back into town, she would hear it or see the headlights through Mickey's windows. Since they had driven west, there were only so many places they could go along the river.

Cash shot a couple games. Drank a couple beers. Smoked a lot of cigarettes. On the third game, she lost on purpose, shrugged, and said, "Guess my game is off tonight. Gonna head back to Fargo, I think."

A couple of the guys who she had been working with for years waved goodbye. One of Svenson's sons tipped his beer bottle and said, "See you in the fields." On the way out, Cash stopped in the bathroom. Everything was dark oak and white porcelain—it reminded her of a horror movie. She did her business and headed out to the truck.

She coasted back out of the parking spot without turning on the ignition or her headlights. No sense giving the guys over at Arnie's any idea of what she was up to if she could help it. She kept the headlights off until she was headed south of the bar and around the corner. She circled the block, turned left and headed toward the river.

Instead of turning down the gravel road that would take her back to the field where Tony O had been thrown, she kept driving west almost to the river bridge. Just before the bridge, she turned north on the road that led to the Bjork farm. Trees lined the river, but to the east were flat fields with the occasional stand of trees that marked a farmstead. Some had the new yard lights. Most didn't.

At night, with no moon, Cash couldn't see much.

At the driveway to the Bjork farm, she turned her headlights off. Anyone watching would think she had turned into the farmstead. Instead, she slowed to a crawl, moving in second gear past the Bjork's, waiting for her eyes to adjust to the dark.

After a couple minutes, she could make out the lane ahead, the fall grass in the ditch a feathery fringe against the edge of the sandy road. She had been down here before and knew it led directly to a wheat field. She could walk across that and arrive directly at where Tony O's body had been thrown out.

She reached the end of the road, put the truck in park and killed the engine. She rolled down the window and listened. Sound carried long distances across the Valley. There were crickets and dogs and the occasional mosquito buzz. She could hear the animals in the Bjork barn moving, making soft animal sounds, almost like humans getting ready for bed. A car turned off the pavement in town onto a gravel road. There were no headlights on this side of town, so it must have been someone going the other direction.

And then she heard men's voices coming across the fields in front of her. A cough. More voices. She looked toward the direction of the voices. She had been right. Their truck was parked in almost the same spot she had parked the Ranchero when she found Wheaton and the feds looking at Tony O's body.

She didn't dare open her door. It would creak and they would hear her shut it. She put on her jean jacket, tucked the cigarette pack and matches that had been on the dash into the front pocket, buttoned it up. She didn't want to waste movement or time once she was out of the truck. She reached behind the seat and grabbed the .22—already loaded, safety on—then pulled out a box of bullets. She took about ten and tucked them in her front jean pocket, right side.

Once she was ready, she stopped and listened some more. Heard the same three voices. She could pick out the voice that she imagined belonged to the young guy named John who had come into Arnie's, but from this distance she couldn't decipher anything they were saying.

When she determined where they were in relation to where she was, she laid the gun on the seat, squatted on the seat, then lifted her left leg out the window. Using the doorframe and steering wheel for balance, she brought out her right leg.

She eased down the side of the truck until her feet touched the ground. She stretched up and reached back inside for her rifle. She looked around to get her

bearings. Right in front of her was the already har-
vested wheat field—nothing but stubble and no cover.

If she was going to approach them by walking
directly across the field, the shortest route, eventually they would see her coming and she would have
nowhere to hide. If she followed the river, she could
come up by the Oye's driveway next to the migrant
shacks, where she had parked the other day, but that
was the long way around. A little closer, but not
directly across was a barbed wire fence that ran south
to north on the Bjork's land. The Bjorks must use that
land as grazing pasture for their cows.

Cash walked into the field and headed directly to
the fence line. She figured if nothing else, with her
short stature and small build, she could freeze as a
fence post if she thought they were suspicious of movement over this way. At the fence, Cash crouched down
and rolled under the barbwire. It was strung in lines of
three along the fence post. Up close she could see the
conductors making at least one of the lines electric. She
remembered as a kid they used to gather a group of
kids from town and line them up by an electric fence,
each touching the shoulder of the kid in front of them.
She or her foster brother would stand at the head of
the line and grab the electric fence. The current would

course through the line of bodies, zapping whichever kid was hooked on at the end of the line. Depending on how strong the farmer had the current set, sometimes the kid would go flying five feet back.

Tonight she avoided the electricity. She stopped every few posts to look in the direction of the pickup. She kept the rifle down along her side, barrel pointed to the ground. There was a cluster of cows along the tree line by the river. She could hear the occasional soft shuffle of one breathing or shifting its weight. The crickets and frogs must have sensed her presence because they had gone quiet, except the ones in the far distance.

The closer she got to the gravel road, the louder and more distinct the men's voices became. As Cash stood silent, becoming the fence pole she was standing next to, she remembered a random science lesson from tenth grade. The teacher had said something about cool air refracting sound waves, which explained being able to hear things better at night. Her body jerked when she heard a couple beer bottles hit the ditch as they got thrown from the truck window.

If it were daylight, both she and the men would have been easily visible to each other, but the men weren't looking for someone to come up on them from the front. They didn't notice when the fence pole fifteen feet in front of them got four inches taller and a few inches thicker.

When the occasional car or truck passed on the road behind them, all three would go quiet, as if anticipating the worst. Once it passed, they resumed talking. The weather. The baseball season. The price of grain on the Grain Exchange. One voice was whiney. The other two were deeper and older. One man was clearly drunk. It wasn't until the brake lights suddenly went on that Cash heard something interesting.

"What the hell!"

"Get your foot off the goddamned brake!"

The whiney voice said, "It was an accident. Move your big shitkickers over so I got some room over here. I don't know why the hell you all had to come back out here anyways."

"Visiting the scene of the crime." The drunk one was talking.

"Shut up!" said the first man.

"Shit, I don't know why you had to go stab him," said the drunk. "He already gave you his check."

Cash was trying to make out the color or make or year of their truck. It was too dark and she was too far away to see the license plate. She could tell you which was an International Harvester dump truck or a Ford grain truck. But damned if she knew the difference between a Ford or Chevy pickup. She loved her Ranchero, which is about all she could tell you about vehicles. Besides, just about every truck in the Valley was dark blue. She was going to have to get closer in order to get Wheaton some useful information.

Damn, she could use a cigarette. And a restroom—all those beers in town were going right through her; she had to pee. She reached over with her left hand and unbuttoned the metal button at the waist of her jeans. There, she could hold it a while longer. She needed to get closer to see the faces of the men in the truck. *What to do?*

Cash came up with a plan. She lay down parallel to the road and tucked the rifle lengthwise against her body, her right arm holding it flat against her. She figured she could roll into the shallow ditch on this side of the road, wait a couple seconds to see if they reacted, then roll across the road into the ditch on the other side. She could use the trees over there as cover to move closer to the truck and try to get a glimpse of their faces.

Just as she rolled under the barbwire and into the first ditch, she heard, "Dumb fucker! I said, keep your goddamn feet off the brake!"

Cash held her breath.

"Next time you tell the whole damn county we're sitting out here, I'll put a bullet through your brain, dumbass."

Cash figured now was a good time to get across the road. In four full rolls, she was there.

Two more rolls brought her to the bottom of the ditch on the other side of the road. Suddenly everything changed. Cash couldn't tell which guy was talking, yelling. They all three went crazy.

"Did you see that bear just run across the road?" one man yelled.

"Ain't no damn bears out here," said another.

"Cut him off," said the man who had threatened to shoot the whiner. Cash thought she was pretty sure of that voice.

"I ain't that drunk. A goddamn bear just ran across the road. Saw it with my own two eyes."

"Maybe it was a raccoon. The river's right there."

Cash lay still, breathing in shallow breaths. All of a sudden, three or four feet in front of her was lit up by a beam from a flashlight.

"What the fuck you doing?" yelled the man who seemed the most sober and angry of the three.

"I told you I saw a goddamn bear. I ain't that damn drunk I don't know what I saw."

When Cash heard the truck door open, she didn't hesitate, she crouched and ran into the trees.

"There! There!" yelled the man. "You can't tell me that ain't no goddamn bear." He was running in her direction, flashlight bobbing with his unsteady weaving.

Whiney-voice was yelling after him, "I got the rifle."

"You stupid fucks, get back here," yelled the first man.

Whiney-voice hollered back, "Get over it, man, anyone asks what we're doing out here, we just say we saw a bear on the road up there and chased it down this way. Come on, let's go find that sucker."

Cash was standing on the river side of a big oak, trying to catch her breath, berating herself for being so stupid as to not at least look at the truck when they first opened the door. She would have been able to see their faces in the dome light. Now she had blown that chance. They had the flashlight. If the beam found her, they would know who she was and hunt her till she was dead. Down this way so close to the river, they would probably just throw her in. Cash worked at calming her breathing. Her rifle was still on safety. She needed to rectify that situation, and soon, 'cause she wasn't ending up like Tony O. Not this girl.

The men were thrashing through the brush and woods, twigs snapping under their feet. Cash held her breath and clicked the safety off. To her ears it was a loud metallic sound, but the men must not have heard it over the breaking twigs. The flashlight beam was coming closer.

Cash had the advantage of knowing this stretch of riverbank. Sometimes she and Wheaton would come down here to catch catfish, going down to the river's edge by following old cow trails. There should be one about five feet ahead.

Cash scanned the woods and ground in front of her, squinting to make the most of the shapes in the dark. When she was as certain as she could be that she wasn't going to run into a dead tree lying across her forward path, she took off in as silent a run as she could manage. The men must have heard something because the flashlight beam scanned her way, barely missing her as she jumped onto the cow path.

They fired off a shot. Cash headed to the river's edge, about forty feet ahead of where the men were. *Shit!* Thank god they'd been drinking—they were just shooting blind. Still, being hunted had her heart racing faster than anyone's should. She could hear one of the guys was yelling at the shooter for firing. From the way their voices carried, Cash could tell they were turning back up the riverbank.

As she got closer to the river's edge, she felt her tennies sinking into the clay. They started to make a slurping sound each time she lifted her foot. Ahead of her was an old elm tree that had died and fallen out across the river. She dropped the rifle on the other side of it and hoisted herself over. The size of the tree hid her from view. She squatted and felt for the .22. It was right there. Thank god it hadn't dropped in the river.

Cash knew she couldn't hold it any longer. After getting shot at, she really needed to pee. She tilted her head to listen. The men were lost way behind her, still farther up on the riverbank. She could hear their voices, could hear them trashing through the underbrush, but she couldn't make out words.

She stood up facing the river. She could tell she was about three feet from the water. She unzipped her jeans and dropped them. As soon as she squatted, she made sure the rifle was about a foot off to her right side and then released her bladder. As her urine hit the cold river clay, warm steam rose up her backside. *What a relief.* She stopped peeing midstream and listened again for the men. It sounded like they were still moving up the riverbank. She started peeing again. Done, she shook her butt, no toilet paper out here, and pulled up her undies and jeans in one yank. She grabbed her rifle, leaned against the tree and listened. The men had given up. She heard the truck doors slam, first one door then the other. But she didn't hear the engine turn over.

Oh, Christ. They were probably gonna sit there and tell bear stories while they finish however much beer they've brought out with them.

Cash had no idea what time it was. But the beer she had earlier, the adrenaline rush of the chase, and the late hour all of a sudden made her extremely tired. Plus, she still had to get to her truck and drive back into Fargo. She couldn't show up in town all covered in river mud or the town talk would reach these three men's ears and they would know it wasn't a bear they were chasing in the woods. And damn, she wanted a cigarette and a drink of plain old water.

Cash climbed back over the fallen tree and walked on the cow path about a quarter mile, stood and listened again. She heard the river water moving upstream, softly slapping mud, but she still hadn't heard the truck engine start. She stepped off the path and headed up the riverbank, coming out of the woods a bit farther up the road from where she had first rolled across it.

Cash didn't take any chances. She could barely make out their truck still sitting down the road. She followed the tree line to the spot where the barbwire fence ran to the river. She decided to risk walking across the cow pasture. She figured if the men were still looking for the bear, they were looking at the woods on the riverside of their truck instead of in her direction anyways. She was tempted to run but had no desire to trip and land in a cow pie and add that mess to the river mud she was already covered in. She got to her truck in about fifteen minutes. From there she could still make out the outline of their truck sitting across the fields.

CASH PUT THE .22 THROUGH the driver's side window. She walked back over to the small ditch and scooped up a handful of damp mud from the bottom to smear across both tail lights. Done, she wiped her hands first on grass and then on her jeans. She hoisted herself up the side of the Ranchero into the truck bed and walked to the front end. From there she sent her right leg into the cab, then her left and slid herself down into the driver's seat. She smelled like cow shit. She crossed her arms on the steering wheel and dropped her head. *Damn reconnaissance mission. Damn.* She could feel her legs and arms quivering, the adrenaline coursing through her body.

Cash took a deep breath and turned on the truck. It sounded like an airplane starting up. The truck across the way stayed put. Cash backed down Bjork's road as far as she could, then eased the Ranchero into their driveway, where she hesitated before deciding she wasn't going to return to Halstad. Instead she made her way to the state bridge and jumped on the North Dakota highway that ran directly into Fargo. She pushed the Ranchero up to eighty and hauled ass. When she could see the red lights and the sweeping blue beam of Hector Airport in North Fargo, she slowed down. The acrid smell of the sugarbeet plant reminded her that in a few more weeks she would be hauling beets nonstop. That would be the major income that would get her through the winter.

She drove through the backstreets of Fargo. Swung by the Casbah just on habit, took a look at the cars and trucks that lined the street. Saw some familiar vehicles and some not familiar.

Jim was there. The backside of his Ford pickup was smashed in where some high school kid, after a winning football game, had backed right into him. Cash wondered what time it was. There was no way she could go inside looking like she did. She'd run home and clean up and, if it wasn't too late, run back down for a couple beers and some Jim.

Cash parked. She grabbed her rifle and ran up the outside stairs to her apartment. The screen door screeched. She put the rifle across the table and looked at the clock sitting next to her bed. Christ, it was only 11:30 at night. Felt more like 3 A.M. But shit, she had plenty of time.

She hustled back down to her truck and grabbed the six-pack that she'd bought earlier. She took one bottle and put the other five, cardboard carrier and all, into the fridge on the top shelf where she supposed most folks kept milk. She popped the top and took a long swig, then lit a cigarette. When she had smoked about half, she set the remainder in the green ashtray—smoke curling toward the heat of the kitchen light that read Holiday Inn. She carried the Bud into the bathroom with her.

As the water filled the tub, Cash stripped.

Damn, she had forgotten about the .22 bullets she had stuffed into her front pocket. A couple shells rolled under the clawfoot bathtub. She would get them later when she cleaned.

Steam rose out of the water. When her body was submerged, steam came up off her also. With a beer in her left hand and a cigarette in her right, she used the toilet for her ashtray.

She lay like that and thought about the night. She never had gotten a good look at any of the men. And because it was so dark she couldn't even began to guess their heights. She knew the whiney guy now, not his name but who he was. What he looked like. The first guy, the one who wasn't drunk—she would be able to recognize his voice. And the drunk guy—that would be a harder guess, unless she happened to be in a bar where he was already drunk and talking.

Cash finished her cigarette and flipped it into the toilet. It hissed as it hit the water. She killed the beer and quickly soaped up, rinsed off and got out of the tub. She dried off and scooped her clothes up from the floor. She cleaned out her jean pockets, laying a couple crumpled one-dollar bills, change and the remaining .22 bullets on the dresser top. She pulled on a clean pair of jeans and T-shirt that had been washed and worn so many times it felt like silk. Her tennis shoes were filthy, full of cow shit. She reached under the bed and pulled out the cowboy boots she usually just wore on Saturday nights when she pretended she was getting dressed up to go out.

ONE OF THE FARMERS HAD hired her to clean out his migrant sheds at the end of beet-hoeing season and she'd found the boots tucked under one of the beds. They were plain old cowboy boots, with plenty of white stitching up the sides in whorls and curlicue things. The foot of the boot was a darker brown, the top almost a creamy white. She imagined these were someone's going-to-Catholic-church boots or going-out-dancing-on-Saturday-night boots. The going-to-church thing was not something she did. Occasionally, she danced around a barroom floor.

She tried on the boots that day in the migrant shed. They slipped on her feet as if they were made for her. She had carried the boots with the broom and dustpan, all grouped together in one hand so that if the farmer looked her way, it would have just looked like she was carrying a pile of rubbish with the broom, not trusting that he wouldn't have taken them from her. She had walked directly to her Ranchero and thrown them in back. The farmer hadn't looked in her direction at all. She went back into the shack and checked under the other bed. No more treasures.

There were four shacks on this property. She went into the other two she had already cleaned and checked under those two beds also. *Nada*. She walked over to the shed the farmer had been working on. It was interesting to her how she had cleaned three and he was just now finishing up with one.

"All done," she told him. He reached into his back pocket and pulled out a roll of bills, peeled off three fives and handed them to her.

"Thanks, Cash. If I need more help I'll leave word at Mickey's, all right?"

"That'll work."

She had gotten into her Ranchero and driven off to Fargo, had tried on her boots again as soon as she got home.

Cash had learned a long time ago that wanting was not something foster kids allowed themselves to do. It had never even occurred to her that she might covet something this pretty. And even when she started to make her own money, she only bought what she needed. That and cigarettes and beer.

TONIGHT CASH PULLED ON THE boots and tucked her jeans into them. She ran a brush through her hair to get the leaves and dirt out of it and pulled it back into a ponytail. She stuffed her keys and cash into her front jean pocket, Marlboros and matches into the other, turned the lock on her apartment door and pulled it shut behind her. The hard leather soles of the boots sounded loud going down her apartment stairs.

The air was early fall warm. Here in town you couldn't see the stars for the streetlights.

Damn. She'd forgotten her cue. This close to closing, there probably wasn't enough time to really play anyways. She walked to the Casbah, catching the screen door with her back foot to give her hair time to follow her in. She smiled to herself as she saw Ole pass his quarter to Clyde.

Shorty had her Bud ready for her. Tonight, ol' man Willie was passed out at a table in back, and damn, given the wide berth around him, he really must have pissed himself.

Jim was shooting pool. He nodded his cue at her. "Want to play partners?"

"Sure."

Jim went around the table to the guy he was shooting against. "My partner's here now," he said. "You and your wife still want to play?"

The guy nodded, walked over to a booth and leaned in.

When his wife slid out across the leather seat, Cash could tell right away she was going to be a sore loser. A little overweight and still poured into her Levi's, she had the country girl ratted-up and hair-sprayed hairdo. She was the kind of white woman who called girls like Cash *squaw*.

Jim didn't notice. Even if he did notice, he wouldn't notice. That's just how things were in the Valley.

The other guy broke. When Jim motioned for Cash to go next, she shook her head no. "You go first," she told him. Cash hoped that Jim would run the table. If he won the game for them, the wife wouldn't be so sore about losing. Jim ran all but three. The wife took her turn. Cash watched her walk around the table, use her cue to line up a shot, then change her mind and lean down to take a different shot. It was clear to Cash the woman was posturing, going through the moves she had seen better pool players make without really knowing why they did them. She did sink two balls, though, before completely miscuing on the third one.

"Clean it up," Jim encouraged Cash. She walked around the table. Balls 9-7-3 and then 8 in the corner. That would be the play. She could see the man's wife scowling at her, her petulance fueled by the beer she was drinking.

"I don't know, Jim," said Cash. "That three is a little hidden."

Jim put his arm around her waist and nuzzled her neck. "Who you trying to kid?" he breathed. "You could make those three shots left-handed and you know it."

Cash gently pushed him away. She ran the 9-7-3 and then put the 8 right in front of her last pocket.

"Choked, huh?" said the wife.

"Happens to the best of us," Cash said, putting chalk on the tip of her cue and walking over to the wall railing, where she had set her beer.

"Come on, John, win us another pitcher," the wife cheered. Her breasts threatened the buttons of her cotton blouse as she leaned into him.

"Back up then and give me a shot," he said. She

pouted her way over to the booth to take a drink from her beer.

"What are you doing?" Jim whispered to Cash. "Those were kindergarten shots."

"She's gonna get pissed if I win this game for us. She doesn't want to be beat by another woman, certainly not an Indian."

"Get off it, Cash. It ain't like that."

"Sure it is. You ain't got anything to complain about anyways. I put the 8-ball right in front of the pocket. All you gotta do is breathe the cue ball by it and it's going to drop in."

All of a sudden they heard, "JOHN! Goddamn it. How could you do that?"

Cash looked at the table and saw where John had put the 8-ball in, losing the game for the couple. Cash grinned at Jim over her Bud bottle.

"Indian bitch." Those were the next words Cash heard.

"What'd you say?" asked Cash.

"Let it go, Cash, let it go." Jim pulled on Cash's arm.

All the old men along the bar had turned around on their barstools and were staring.

"No white chick's gonna call me names just 'cause she can't shoot pool," Cash retorted. Jim grabbed the cue stick and beer bottle out of her hand as Cash moved around the table toward the woman.

"She isn't worth it, Cash," Jim pleaded.

"What'd you say?" said the advancing Cash. "You want to say that again?"

The woman's husband stepped between the two women. "She's drunk," he told Cash.

The woman sneered, "Not that damn drunk."

Cash slipped behind the man and slapped the woman across the face with an open right palm. When the woman gasped, Cash hauled back and hit her square in the solar plexus with her left. "You ain't worth my time, bitch," she breathed out hard.

Jim grabbed Cash and pulled her back. "Come on, we're leaving."

"Get your fucking hands off me," hollered Cash, trying to break free.

The man was hurriedly telling his wife to get her shit together and get the hell out. She was crying, her mascara running in rivulets down her chubby cheeks.

"Yeah, get her outta here before I kick her sorry ass," taunted Cash.

All talk had gone quiet in the bar, with Charlie Pride once again trying to get to San Antone. It was so quiet you could hear the TV announcer describing the seventh inning of that night's Twins' game. No drinks were being lifted and set down. No one moved. The man, his arm wrapped around his wife's thick waist, led her out of the bar. Jim let go of Cash and handed her the cue stick. He turned and picked up his own stick, broke it down and started putting it in its carrying case.

"Stupid bitch," said Cash. "Come on, we got the table to ourselves. May as well play till last call." She put some quarters into the money slot, pushed it in and the balls fell down. She racked the balls and stood looking at Jim. The rest of the bar had gone back to serious murmuring. Cash heard her name whispered a couple times but let it go. Her hands were shaking with unused adrenaline.

"Stupid bitch," she repeated, running six balls in a row until she scratched the cue ball.

"Let it go, Cash," pleaded Jim as he ran four balls and then missed his shot.

Cash hated when he got all wishy-washy. In fact, she was damn sick and tired of everyone ignoring fucking reality. A man was dead, an Indian man. His wife was drinking and there were babies involved, babies who more likely than not would get taken away from the woman if she kept on that way.

She looked at Jim. His pale skin. His blond hair combed back. His forearms tan from working in the fields. He wasn't that many years older than her but he would inherit acres from his daddy's farm. Acres given free to his immigrant granddaddy. Probably stolen from her granddaddy. No matter how much she loved this Valley, no one was going to give her a homestead, not after they'd already stolen it from her. In that moment, she hated his whiteness.

"Let what go, Jim? The dead Indian in the field that some white guys killed for his truck-driving money? The seven children that don't have a daddy anymore? Just what the fuck am I supposed to let go of, Jim?" Cash pointed her cue at the center pocket to her left, indicating that was where she was going to cut the 8-ball. She made the shot and said, "Rack 'em up. And get me another beer."

"Maybe we should quit," Jim said.

"Maybe you should rack 'em up and get me another beer." Cash saw that Shorty already had another bottle open on the bar for her. She pointed with her stick for Jim to go pay for it. Jim obliged and Cash broke the rack, making two balls, one stripe and one solid. She made another stripe before missing a long shot. She gulped the beer when Jim handed it to her. "Have at it," she said to Jim.

They played each other until closing time. Apparently no one else in the bar wanted to take either one of them on. Cash knew Jim didn't blame them. He was shooting sloppy, worried about her drinking and her anger. *Fuck him and the white horse he rode in on.*

Shorty called out, "Last call." Last chance to buy a beer. Fifteen minutes to drink up the one in your hand.

Cash used the tip of her cue to push the 8-ball into the nearest pocket. She walked up to the bar and ordered two Buds, then sat on a barstool and proceeded to drink, first a gulp from one bottle and then a gulp from another.

Jim nursed the last half of the beer he had gotten two games ago. Cash could tell he was nervous about how much she was drinking. *Fuck him.*

When she had killed the two bottles, she stood up, put the bar cue back in the wall rack and started to walk out, lifting a hand in a semi-wave to the regulars still hanging out. She felt Jim follow her. He didn't speak at all on the walk back to her apartment. She was feeling the effects of all the beer she had drunk. Also, come to think of it, when was the last time she had eaten? *Shit.*

She used the railing of the staircase to steady herself. She fumbled in her jeans for her key and waved at the air a few times before catching the light chain above the kitchen table. Jim raised his eyebrows when he saw the .22 sitting on the kitchen table.

"Rabbit hunting," Cash mumbled. She went to the fridge and brought out two beers. Opened one and handed it to Jim and opened the other one for herself, taking a long drink as she plopped on the edge of the overstuffed chair and tried to pull her boots off. Jim saw her struggle and bent down to help get them off. He set them neatly on the floor. Somehow that made Cash giggle.

"What?"

"Nothin'." She stripped off her shirt, dropped her jeans and undies on the floor in front of her, picked up her beer and crawled into bed. Jim stood next to the bed and Cash watched him take his shirt off and throw it over the back of the chair. Next, she heard his jeans hit the floor. Actually she heard the *thud* of his wallet in his jeans pocket hit the floor. She giggled again. She never understood why he always left his underwear on until he was under the covers.

"What now?" he asked.

"Nothin'." She rolled to face him and pulled his head toward her to kiss him. "Nothin' at all."

When they were finished, she rolled to her edge of the bed, reached down for her beer and lit a cigarette. She pushed the pillow up behind her back for cushion as she sat up, pulling the sheet up far enough to cover her breasts, holding it tucked under her armpits. She giggled once more. She could do modesty too.

"Are you laughing at me?"

"Nah, just thinking of that crazy fat lady in the bar."

"What the hell set you off? She's not the first woman to make some stupid remark, doubt she'll be the last."

"Yeah, well, that might be the problem. No one is ever the last."

"What'd you mean about some white guys killing an Indian? You talking about that guy who got killed up by Halstad?"

"Yeah."

"He has kids?"

"Yeah."

"How you know that?"

"My cousin's husband." Cash took another drink to quell the giggle she felt rising. Damn, who would have thought she had a big family. Even a pretend cousin was more than she had before Tony O died in a field. Sadness came in a wave as she pictured the baby in the swing and the little girl sitting on the bed, gently pushing her baby sister back and forth. She could see Josie drinking the whiskey from the jelly glass. "Fuck." Cash took another drink of her own beer. "Damn."

"What's up, Cash? You're thinking too hard."

"Time for you to get home to your wife and kids, Jim." He tried to kiss her neck, ran his hands down her side.

"Nah, go on now. It's late. Go on. I got things I got to do tomorrow and you got a wife cooking you breakfast. Get to getting."

Cash lit another cigarette and smoked as she watched Jim dress in the dim lights coming in from outside. She smiled to herself thinking of how he had pulled his underwear on under the covers before getting out of bed. When he came around to her side of the bed, he leaned down and she raised her face to his for a goodbye kiss.

"Lock the door handle on your way out, okay?" she said, the way she'd said dozens of times before.

"Will do."

CASH HEARD THE DOOR CLICK behind him and then the screen as he eased it shut. She lay in bed, thinking of the run through the woods, the men who had chased a bear, the woman who hated her without knowing her, Josie and her children, Tony O lying dead in the field. Josie and Tony O's winter dreams running with his blood into the Red River topsoil, and then on into the Red River, flowing north to all that is cold.

Fuck!

Cash rolled out of bed and pulled on her clothes along with a hooded sweatshirt under her jean jacket. She opened her top dresser drawer and felt around for the sock where she stashed her money. She rolled a bill off the wad and stuffed it in her jeans pocket, grabbed her truck keys off the kitchen table and went down the stairs.

The only restaurant open would be in Moorhead. Cash crossed the bridge and drove south, past Moorhead State College and Concordia, the college for blond, blue-eyed Norwegians and Swedes. She pulled into Shari's Kitchen, an all-night truck stop that served breakfast 24 hours.

The light inside the restaurant was glaring. Judging from the disjointed conversations and the sullen or over-animated faces, she wasn't the only drunk who craved a protein fix to stall the morning hangover. She grabbed a stool at the counter. The waitress put a cup of coffee in front of her. "What can I get you, hon? Kinda chilly out there tonight, huh?"

"The truckers' special. Not too bad, gonna get a lot colder pretty soon."

"You want some orange juice with that?"

"I guess." She picked up the *Fargo-Forum* that was lying on the counter a few stools down. She scanned the front page without seeing anything about the killing thirty miles north. Guess a dead Indian wasn't newsworthy. She turned the paper to Ann Landers and read Ann's advice to some poor soul who was worried about women's liberation ruining her relationship with her husband. By the time her eggs and pancakes arrived, Cash had read through the paper and was looking over the funnies.

She ate her food absentmindedly. Years ago she had gotten bored with life's necessities—food, sleep, comfort. Now she ate when she remembered to. Slept because she had to. And comfort? *Hmmmm.* During her years in foster homes, it was all she could do just to get through to the next day. She had gotten good at getting through.

She drank the last of her orange juice and coffee,

put a five-dollar bill on the table on top of her check, then zipped up the sweatshirt and buttoned the two bottom buttons of her jean jacket. She nodded to the waitress as she left the restaurant.

Cash drove through Moorhead, went back over the bridge to her apartment, stripped and climbed into bed. She was asleep before she could even think of drinking the last of the beer that sat on the bed stand or light a last cigarette.

SHE BECAME AWARE THAT SHE was dreaming even as the woman appeared before her. She listened, careful to pay attention. It was Josie Day Dodge. She stood at the end of Cash's bed, wearing the same clothes Cash had last seen her in. Her hair was falling down her back in two braids hooked together at the ends. She was holding ribbons in her hands. On closer look, Cash saw that they were strands of wiigob, the strands of basswood that were used to tie birchbark together to make baskets. Josie was running the basswood through her hands. She looked at Cash and said, "I have to go make more baskets. Tell the kids I have to go. That I'll make more baskets. They can sell the baskets with the pinecones. I've got to go. Tony O hasn't come home yet. Make sure they don't mess with his body."

She pushed her hands through the basswood strips, her fingers sorting through the long strips the way Cash ran her fingers through her dried hair. She faded.

When Cash opened her eyes, it was 5:00 A.M. She swung her legs over the edge of the bed and sat up, holding the bedsheet and blanket up around her, over her shoulder and across her chest and midriff. With her one free arm, she sifted through the ashes and butts in the ashtray until she found three-quarters of a butt.

There were times after dreams like that when she knew that someone else was dead. Shit, she hated this. She didn't know anyone else who was visited by folks who were dead or dying or just passing through on the night air. *Fuck*.

Now she would need to take another trip up to Red Lake. See where those two little ones were. Damn, she'd never even met the older kids. She reached down for her crumpled pack of cigarettes out of her jacket and lit another one.

Cash didn't leave much room in her heart for feelings. She had learned a long time ago to squash those little buggers down. But thinking about Josie and Tony O's kids made her chest feel tight. In every school she had attended, each grade seemed to have an Indian kid from a foster home—a kid working someone's fields or doing their laundry for them so their wife and kids would look good in church on Sunday morning.

Cash had learned that friendships were fleeting. The county moved foster kids around at the slightest provocation. And rarely were brothers and sisters kept together. She had no idea where hers were. The Indian kids played together on the playground and talked about how the social worker would show up one day, stuff them in a car and take them to some new place. Some of their parents drank, some of them were just poor, but the common denominator was they were all Indian. Legal kidnapping.

White parents drank. White parents were poor. Heck, some of them beat the crap out of their kids on a weekly basis. No social worker ever drove up and stuffed their kids in a car.

Cash had never met a white foster kid, come to think of it. A deep drag on the cigarette. She had waited for years for her mother to come get her. The beatings, the touches in the middle of the night, the food used as punishment, as reward. The cold parsnips—after a night of sitting sleepily in the kitchen chair and not being able to gag them down, the foster mother, with the aid of her biggest daughter, had forced them down her throat before church on Sunday morning. No matter what the social worker said or the foster mother screamed, Cash knew this was not the life her mother had planned for her, and that somewhere her mom was sitting, smoking, just like Cash now was—although her preferred brand was Camels—her heart as thick and heavy as Cash's.

Cash had never felt abused or unloved by her mom. She had missed her brother and sister so bad at first it made her sick, unable to think straight, a constant fog in her brain. As the years wore on she had adapted, called on something to get her through each day, each moment. She had learned to not ask about her mom, her brother, her sister. Because when she did ask, she was told her mom didn't want her, that her brother and sister had forgotten her. She didn't believe any of that. But she gave up hope, because hope created more pain.

And now a whole family of kids was going to experience the same thing, she just knew it.

Cash walked into the kitchen and picked up another crumpled pack of Marlboros she had thrown on the table. She took one out and lit it up as she prepared some coffee. She stood smoking, looking at the morning darkness out her kitchen window while she waited for her coffee to boil.

Once done, she sat down at the table, still wrapped in the sheet. Her mind caught the image of Josie standing at the end of her bed, the wiigob running through her fingers. Cash wondered how a mother could ever choose to leave her children, but the thought made her colder than the linoleum floor had made her feet and she chased it away by taking a sip of the too-hot coffee. She took a few more sips, then got up to finish getting dressed.

This time she knew she was taking a trip. She made her bed quilt into a long strip by folding it lengthways by thirds, laid a pair of jeans length-wise on the quilt strip, then a T-shirt. Last a pair of undies and clean socks. She rolled the whole thing up into a log-sized roll and slipped a belt around it to clinch it tight.

Back at the kitchen table, she remembered the .22 bullets that had rolled under the bathtub. She went into the bathroom and retrieved them from where they rested on the far underside baseboard, then stuffed them back in her front jean pocket. She went back out to the kitchen table, made sure the .22 was loaded and the safety was on. At the sink she rinsed the river clay and cow shit off the bottom of her tennies as best she could.

The sky was starting to lighten by the time she was ready to walk out the door. She debated on getting the beers still left in the six-pack but decided she could always stop along the way to pick up more if she needed to. It was a good thing she had eaten last night, she thought.

Once in her truck she headed north to Ada. She would catch Wheaton just when he was arriving at the jail.

He was at the clerk's desk, talking on the phone with someone who wanted him to take the names of some kids who were stealing from her store. Wheaton dutifully wrote down their names on a pad of paper only to crumple it into a ball and toss it into the wastebasket sitting by the desk after hanging up.

"Those Stevenson kids been stealing since they could walk through the store themselves. All they ever take is candy. If they had some food at home, they wouldn't be walking into town to steal sugar to eat. Whatever happened to Christian charity?" he muttered. "You didn't see that. Or hear it," he said to Cash. "Got anything new?"

Cash slumped into the chair that sat next to the desk. "Almost got shot last night."

"What!"

"Not quite." Cash laughed. "They had one too many drinks to know what they were doing. Fact of the matter is, they thought they were shooting at a bear."

"What the hell. What were you up to?"

Cash told him the story of going to the two town bars and then figuring that the men had gone back to the field where Tony O's body had been dumped. How she had gone down by the Bjork farm, tromped through fields and then ended up getting chased because they thought she was a bear.

This morning it was funny. She had a hard time telling Wheaton the story without laughing—the hold-your-stomach, tears-roll-down-your-cheeks kind of laugh—talking some, then getting overcome with silliness again. She could tell from Wheaton's face he didn't find it funny at all.

Gasping for breath she said, "Damn, Wheaton, I'm sorry. I can't even tell you what kind of truck they were in. You know I can't tell the difference between a Ford and a Chevy. It was dark, I know that. It was dark-colored."

More laughter.

"And I saw the one guy in Arnie's bar. The other

two, one was drunk, one wasn't. But they were talking about killing Tony O."

Finally, the laughter was dying down. Cash knew that most of it was the nervous energy she didn't get to burn off last night. She had been hunted as a bear and dealt with some stupid white broad when she had had far too many beers to think straight. She wasn't going to tell Wheaton that story though.

Trying for a serious face, she said, "Best I can tell you, Wheaton, is to listen around town for whoever was out hunting bear last night."

"You don't want to hang around tonight and see who's talking?" Wheaton asked her.

All the funny left Cash. "Nah. I gotta go back up to Red Lake."

"Red Lake?"

"Yeah, I dreamt last night Tony O's wife died. You know if his body got sent up there yet?"

"What was the dream?"

Cash told him about Josie standing at the end of her bed, running her fingers through the basswood strands, telling Cash she had to go. Wheaton leaned back in his chair, folded his hands across his middle and just looked at her.

He stood up. "Let's go check. Ride with me."

They walked out to his cruiser. Cash rolled down the window and lit up a cigarette. "What?" she asked.

"The call before the store clerk . . . It was a call from the feds up Bemidji way. When the priest went out to the Day Dodge place to ask the wife what she wanted done for a burial, he found the kids in a state."

"She was going to bury him the old way," Cash said quietly.

"The kids were crying. Screaming. Huddled in one of the back bedrooms. Seems their ma had drunk herself to death overnight. By the time the tribal police got back ahold of the feds, all the bigger kids had disappeared. Their dad's boat is still on the shore, so they figure the kids are out in the woods. Got a couple trappers, hunters out looking for them. But you know what I think. Indians looking for Indians, even if they find them, they aren't going to turn them over to no state social workers. Got the little ones, apparently a little girl and a baby, staying at their auntie's house down the road, from what they told me."

Cash slumped in her seat.

"Foster homes are bad for kids," she said finally. "You know that, Wheaton."

"Maybe that auntie will take care of them."

"Like the county gave me to my aunties? There are

seven kids, Wheaton. Seven. You think one of these farmers around here is ready to take in seven Indians? Nah, they'll be split up and shipped all over the state."

Cash stared out the window, then turned to Wheaton. "You know, every one of these farmers is farming our land. They got it for free. The government gave them our land for free." Cash was almost yelling at Wheaton. "And now they'll have seven more farm laborers to work our land for them . . . for free!" She slammed her hand on the dash and turned back away from him.

They drove in silence for the couple blocks until Wheaton pulled into the hospital parking lot. Cash jumped out, slammed the car door and stomped to the entrance. She waited there for Wheaton, glaring off into space. When he caught up with her, they made their way down into the basement that seemed even colder than the time they visited just a couple days ago.

Dr. Felix was sitting at his desk. Feet up on it. Reading the *Fargo Forum*. When he saw Cash and Wheaton, he slid his feet to the floor, slowly, as if to say to them, *Your presence isn't why I'm doing this.*

"What can I do you for you, Sheriff? Got another body for me?"

"Wondering where Tony O's body is," said Wheaton.

"Should have gotten into Red Lake last night," said the doc. "Some injuns from the tribe came down yesterday morning, loaded him in a box on the back of a pickup truck. That's the last I seen of 'em."

Cash and Wheaton turned to go.

"What? That's all you wanted to know?" the doc asked their retreating backs.

Cash lit up another cigarette as soon as they got out of the hospital. "Like I said, don't let me die there. And hell, if I get sick and need a doctor, if I get shot or something, drive me into Fargo, all right?"

"All right. Listen, doesn't seem like you need to go up to Red Lake. What more can you do? It's just gonna upset you. You don't really know the family, you're not from there."

"I know. But it's the dream. I gotta go. Whether I want to or not."

"What are you going to do once you get there?"

"I don't know. I can't just leave it alone. I don't know why I dream these things. See things. Don't ask. I just know I got to go. I don't know why she came to me. Figure I'll know when I get up there what I need to say or do. Say something to her kids at least." Cash slumped against the car door.

She looked like the little kid he had carried into his jail all those years ago. He reached over and touched her shoulder. They drove in silence the few short blocks back to her Ranchero.

Before she got out of the cruiser, Wheaton said, "You know, you don't have to work farms all your life."

Cash looked at him, her eyebrows raised.

"I don't know, you were the smartest kid all through school. Seems you could be doing something besides driving grain truck."

"Yeah. Okay." Cash pulled the door handle.

"I'll stop at the bars at noon and nose around. See if anyone in town has been talking about bears down by the river. Drive careful, hear?"

"You bet," said Cash. She walked to her truck, got in and headed north.

SUN-DRENCHED WHEAT FIELDS. HEALING RAYS *of god's love wash gently over me.* Oh, hell, thought Cash, as she turned the country station on as loud as she could handle. She supposed someday she'd have to write that down. The bottom drawer of her dresser was almost filled with notepads of—what? Poems?

Songs? Had never occurred to her to think about what it was she was writing. But the words would come into her head and run through her brain waves until she put them on paper. Once they were written down, they quit popping up through her consciousness. Time to do it for this one because god's love wasn't doing her or anyone else all that much good.

The news came on the radio station. Apparently the VC were presenting an eight-point peace plan and then something about the Paris Peace talks still being at a stalemate. Meanwhile the body count rose. Cash had had her fill of getting shot at. Not something she wanted to face on a nightly, hourly basis. No thanks. She wanted a drink so bad. Didn't make sense though. Instead, she pulled off the main road where she could see no farmers were out plowing or combining. She drove about a quarter of a mile onto a mud field road, got out of her truck, pulled the rifle from behind the seat. She walked the small ditch for a few yards, finding three empty beer bottles along the way.

She set the bottles on top of three fence posts, with four fence posts between each one.

She opened the driver's door of her truck, rested the rifle through the open window, then proceeded to fire off bullets until the three beer bottles were shattered glass. Not that bad, she thought. *But not that good either*. With eight bullets she'd eventually hit all three bottles. She put a new bullet in the chamber and the safety back on the gun.

She put it back behind her seat and sat there watching a few birds fly. The white clouds drifted across the sky. Smoking. Not really thinking about anything. Just sitting. She could smell the earth, the combined field she sat next to. Thank god she drank. She really didn't know how she'd get through life any other way.

She had gotten over missing her mom, her brother and her sister years ago. Or at least she thought she had. Wheaton was her only real friend. Jim didn't count. She should have whacked him with the cue stick last night. Always trying to appease folks. *Come on, Cash, let it go*. Yeah, she figured that's how folks ended up dead. Just letting it go. Well, so far she had had to let go of everyone who mattered to her. Maybe she didn't want to *just let it go* anymore.

Maybe she should have stopped Josie from drinking the other day.

Cash thought about how in the past, without knowing it, she would find herself scanning the cabs as the beet trucks or grain trucks lined up in the fall, looking at the drivers, never quite admitting to herself she was looking for her ma.

The only time she had ever walked into a church willingly was once around Christmas a few years back. She had seen a couple of Indian women getting out of a car driven by a white social-worker-type woman. The women each had a grocery bag and they walked into the church. Their dark calico-flowered skirts hung down to their ankles. They were wearing shoes, while the social worker lady had on some kind of fancy zip-up boots with fur trim around the top that were made to go over the high heels she was wearing.

The Indian women had kerchiefs tied around their heads and knotted under their chins. Old wool coats hung loosely down their shoulders and backs. Cash had never seen her mother dressed in a skirt, but maybe she had aged and gotten Jesus. Maybe one of those women was one of the aunties who used to fake-speak Spanish to get into the bars.

Cash had looked at the church sign and read that the Lutheran church was having a holiday bazaar, selling beadwork made by Indians from the White Earth Reservation. Cash had driven around town for about fifteen minutes, then pulled up to the church. When she walked in, there was no one upstairs. Just empty rows of pews facing the dead guy hanging on the cross up front. Creepy. She could hear voices in the church basement so she walked down the wooden stairs behind the last row of pews. At the bottom of the stairs she looked into the church kitchen area. The Indian women were laying out beaded earrings and tiny leather moccasins on two of the dining tables.

Neither of the women was Cash's ma nor an auntie. Cash didn't even remember if she felt disappointed or not. She just turned and walked back up the stairs and out of the church.

Cash finished her cigarette, stubbed it out in the ashtray. She turned the key in the ignition, backed around and continued her drive north to Red Lake.

IT WAS EARLY AFTERNOON WHEN she pulled into Josie's driveway. No one was in sight. Cash got out of the truck and walked up to the house. No child answered her knock, but Cash felt like she was being watched. She looked around but didn't see any movement that would tell her where whoever it was, was. The birds were silent, so someone had to be around.

Cash walked around the corner of the house and down the path that led to the shore. The traps and fishing nets hung lifeless from the trees. Even the boat already looked forlorn. Sadness permeated the air. Cash stood at the lakeshore and looked out onto the expanse of Red Lake.

Stories told said that there had been a battle between the Ojibwe people and the Dakota. It was such a bloody battle it turned the lake water red. Cash stood there and felt ancient grief wrap itself around the present-day sorrow. The water lapping the sand did so with sorrow. The leaves moving in the gentle wind off the lake moved with sorrow.

Cash stood there silently until the birds started to talk to each other again. Until the insects started to fly through the air again. Wrapped in a fog of grief, it was her subconscious that registered the sound—though maybe it wasn't even a sound, maybe it was just an undercurrent of awareness that off to her left, in the woods, were humans.

She came back to her physical body, bent down and picked up a small rock that was at her feet. She turned it over and over in her hand, her ears adjusting to the new-felt sounds and sensations that were coming to her. Without looking toward them, she put the stone in her pocket and walked in that direction. There, around the front end of the boat, was a trampled path that led into the woods that lined the shore. Head down, hands in pockets, she followed the path.

The farther she walked, the more silent the woods became. No birds. No insects. Only the soft whap-whap of the lake water hitting the shoreline in the distance.

And then, *bam!* Cash was tackled from behind. She didn't have time to catch herself falling or strike back. Both arms were pulled behind her back. Then she was dragged by hands her size or smaller deeper into the woods and finally plopped against a tree.

It was from that vantage point that she was able to fully see her captors. Surrounding her were five children. She guessed they were somewhere between the ages of ten and fifteen or sixteen. Two looked like twins. Three boys. Two girls. All looked angry, sad, scared and determined. They looked at each other a number of times before the oldest girl said, "Who are you? Why were you bothering our ma?" One of the younger boys kicked Cash on her anklebone. Cash had to breathe deep to not yell out in pain or kick the kid right back.

She took her time. Looking each one in the eyes. They all had the same black eyes as their mom. Now even blacker with sorrow and rage. They were a motley crew. Some wearing pants too big, one of the boys wearing a shirt a size too small. No socks on any of their feet inside their shoes. Only two of them were wearing jackets. The others were layered with undershirts and shirts.

"Didn't you hear me?" asked the girl. Her questions seemed to egg on her little brother, but Cash saw the kick coming this time and swung her legs out of the way before he could connect with bone again.

"I was there where your dad died," she said.

"You hurt my dad?" one of the little ones whispered.

"God, no!" said Cash. "I went out there after he died. After I heard about someone dying."

Two of the kids had tears running down their cheeks. "So what?" asked the girl.

"Well, I talked with the county sheriff. After that, I decided to drive up this way and see if I could be of any help."

"Some help. You got my mom drunk."

"No, I did not! I did not! I tried to let her know easy about your dad. That's all I did. And I held the baby when the white guys came to talk to her. She started drinking right after they left and before I even came out of the bedroom."

"She's dead too."

They all crowded around Cash. Cash was having a hard time tracking who was who. The one who had just talked had tears running down her cheeks and she had her arms wrapped around her midriff, holding in her deepest grief.

"I'm sorry, kids," said Cash in a soft voice. "I'm sorry."

"What you got to be sorry about?" one of the boys asked belligerently. "Your folks aren't dead, leaving you all alone. Our aunt already took the two little ones. Folks been tromping through these woods trying to find us. We aren't going anywhere. I'm not going to any white foster home. I'll die out here myself 'fore I'll let them take me."

A chorus of *me too*'s echoed through the woods.

Cash listened as they told story after story of one cousin or another being taken by social workers and never being seen again. Of best friends going for a ride in the black county Buick and never returning. The kids repeating over and over that the social workers weren't going to get them and split them up.

"Winter's coming," Cash said. "You can't hide out in these woods forever."

"Wanna bet? Our mom and dad were in boarding

schools. They ran away and hid in the woods along the road, all the way from South Dakota until they made it home back here. They taught us what to do if anyone tries to take us. Further up is our maple sugar camp. When the sap runs, we camp out no matter how much snow is on the ground."

Another kid added, "Our dad would take us deer hunting with him. We know these woods like the back of our hands."

"We know how to take care of ourselves. And each other." Another chorus of *yeah*s and *yep*s.

"What about the wake? Don't you want to be there for the ceremony?"

The girl spoke this time. "They told my ma, the last time at the Indian Hospital, that if she drank again, she'd die. Like my brother said, we aren't going in. The social workers will be waiting at the wake to scoop us up. If you're out here to try and get us to go in, you can just leave the same way you came."

"I'm not here to make you go to a foster home. I just came back up when I heard about your mom. I was worried about you all."

"Worried?" one of the kids snorted.

"Yeah, and to see if there was something I could do to help you. Must be something you need."

"What happened to our dad?" asked the girl.

"Can I sit up and get a smoke? You all are making me nervous."

"You should be nervous," growled the kicker.

"You got cigarettes?" asked one of the older boys.

"Yeah. In my back pocket."

"Go ahead, Googoosh," the girl said. "Let her smoke."

Cash thought, *Well, at least I know one name*. At that moment the kicker pulled back his leg to kick her again. His big sister grabbed his arm saying, "Come on, Geno. Give it a break."

Two names.

"What happened to our dad?" said the girl again, still holding her brother. The hold had gone from one of control to comfort. He leaned into his sister, his shoulders shaking with silent sobs. "And give us a couple cigarettes."

Cash dug in her back pocket and pulled out the crumpled pack. She straightened out two and handed them to the girl. Then she straightened out one for herself and lit it before handing the book of matches to the girl. Cash smoked, being careful where she dropped her ashes, using her hand to sweep the ground to bare dirt and using the scooped-out space as an ashtray. She watched the bigger boy light up one and share it with the other boy about his size.

The oldest girl smoked a cigarette by herself. Cash herself had started sneaking cigarettes from a foster father's pack when she was just a kid. She certainly wasn't going to try and reprimand this crew.

Instead she asked, "What have folks told you?"

"That he was shot and they don't know who did it," Googoosh answered.

Another chorus of voices—

"Dumped in a field."

"Killed by a white guy."

"They don't know who shot him."

"Took all his money."

"Money was supposed to get us a Christmas this year."

"That's what Mama said."

"So, you say you were there. What happened?" asked the girl.

"I heard it on the news when I was getting ready to go to work. I work the fields down there full-time. When I heard it, I knew right where it was 'cause I've worked that field, driving combine. The county sheriff was already there."

One of the younger kids said, "She talks like the white girls in Bemidji town."

"Sh!" said one of the other kids.

"She does," said Geno. "She sounds like that snooty white girl at Woolworth's who's always accusing someone of having stolen candy in their pockets."

"How come you talk like a white girl?" asked the girl.

Cash shrugged. "'Cause I live and work with them," she said.

"So where you from?" asked the tallest boy.

"White Earth. But I ended up in foster homes."

"See."

"That's what happens to everyone."

"They're not going to get me."

"So, our dad . . . ?" repeated the girl over the voices.

"When I got there, to the field, the feds were already talking to the sheriff. When I saw the man was Indian like me, I decided to drive up this way, try to talk with your mom, break it easy to her. That's what I tried to do. He had a Red Lake baseball program in his pocket so I knew he was from up here," Cash said. She looked around at the children. They were determined in their resistance. Clearly they knew how the system worked, knew what was in their future. "There's nothing easy about folks dying."

There was a round of nodded heads. Sad looks. Cash's butt was getting damp from sitting on the ground. "Hey, kids, why don't we go back to your house?"

A round of *no way*'s went up.

Cash held up a hand. "Look. The tribal police have already been by, right? The feds and social workers too, right? Your mom told the feds I was her cousin, so if someone comes to the door, you all can just hide and I'll answer."

"Why?"

"'Cause my butt is getting cold. And come on, you need to eat. You need some rest. The best place to get that is at home."

"We don't have a home anymore," one of the kids said. "You just want the social workers to come get us."

"No, I'm not going to turn you in." She saw the distrust in their eyes. "I was in foster homes myself. You don't want to go; I won't be the one to make you go. Come on now, help me up."

The oldest girl leaned down, her long black braid whapping Cash's face as she helped her up from the ground. Cash pulled her jeans down over her ankles and stood up, brushing the dirt and leaves off her backside.

"Let's go," said the girl. "But be quiet. Geno and Googoosh, run up ahead and see if anyone's around the place. We'll come in slower. If you see anyone, run back, don't holler."

The two kids took off. Silent. If you didn't know they were out there, you would never hear them. The rest of the group walked slowly and quietly down a barely perceptible trail. The two younger ones were back shortly, waving their hands. *Come on.* They turned and ran back toward the house. The girl picked up speed and Cash and the other two big kids matched her. Within minutes they could see the house from the tree line. Nothing was moving. The two younger children darted up the wooden steps. Cash heard the door squeak, then saw their two faces in the kitchen window. *All clear.*

The quartet stepped out of the woods and walked up to the house. Cash could feel their bodies strung on high alert, their eyes scanning all directions at once, looking for a trap, listening for any human sound. It wasn't until they were in the house, with the front door shut and a wooden chair propped under the door handle as a lock, that they relaxed a tiny bit.

"Can you tell me your names? So I'm not saying, *hey you*," Cash asked.

The girl pointed at herself, "Mary Jane. Junior (pointing to the tallest boy), Geno (next tallest boy) and this is Squirrel." She pulled the smallest boy close to her.

Cash figured Mary Jane had mothered this one for many years.

"And she's Googoosh," Mary Jane said, pointing at the smallest girl before adding, "Don't turn on the lights. And one of you go open the back bedroom window." Looking at Cash, she said, "If anyone comes down the driveway or up from the lake, we're jumping out that window and heading back into the woods."

Cash shrugged. She walked over to the fridge and opened it. The inside was spotless, the walls and shelves scrubbed clean. Not much food, but some. Jelly, smoked fish, an open tin can of government surplus commodity chicken, with the lid left on top. With the door opened, she turned and looked at Mary Jane. "I can't cook," she said.

Mary Jane walked over to stand beside her. "We could have the fish. I'll mix up some frybread. Just dump that chicken in a pan and heat it up." With that Mary Jane got busy. She became a mini-Josie, scooping flour into a bowl, throwing in some baking soda, salt, some milk. Mixing it into a ball of dough.

She opened the oven and pulled out a cast-iron frying pan that was half-filled with solidified lard. She put it on the front burner, turned it on. After a few minutes, she reached behind her and got her hand wet under the kitchen sink. She flicked some water into the grease. Waited a bit more. Tried again. This time the grease sizzled. At that point, she broke off a ball of dough, formed it into a squat round mass with a finger hole in the middle and dropped it in the grease.

And another, and another, until seven pieces of frybread were floating and frying in the skillet. She reached behind her again, the kitchen as familiar to her as the woods had been, opened a drawer and got a dinner fork. She used the fork to lift the frybread to check its color. When it was the right shade of golden brown, she flipped each one over and watched them fry, left hand on her hip, occasionally using her forearm to swipe back the strands of hair that fell across her face.

While she was doing that, Cash looked through the cupboards. The lower ones were filled with the commodity food the government distributed to reservation families. Canned chicken, beef, tomato juice, dried milk, dried white beans.

Ah, there were canned plums and peaches. Cash pulled out a can of plums, then dug around some more to find a saucepan. She dumped the open can of commod chicken from the fridge into the pan and set it on the stove to simmer. She knew she couldn't handle eating it. It looked like the dog food Wheaton fed his dog, Skip. So she pulled out the smoked fish. When the food was set out on the table—warm frybread, steaming chicken, the commod plums—the kids and Cash all sat down to eat.

Initially there was silence as they all chowed down. As their hunger eased, they started to talk, one after the other, telling stories about their mom and dad. The time they both got drunk one Christmas and knocked over the Christmas tree 'cause they were kissing and lost their balance. The time they were out fishing and their mom got all excited 'cause she saw a walleye jump and she stood up to point and tipped the whole boat over. How every time she had a baby, their dad was there to get a ride for her into the Indian Health Services hospital even though she always swore he was going to miss the delivery.

Cash felt her own sadness, her own loss for her

family. The kids laughed. Sometimes tears slid down their cheeks. How their dad had made the winning home run at the Indian baseball tournament. How their mom beaded tiny moccasins and sold them at the store in the town of Red Lake.

As they talked, the sun dropped in the sky. They still didn't turn on any lights. Just sat around the kitchen table in the coming darkness. They talked about how they would look out for each other. How Mary Jane would send the younger ones to school. How they'd sell pinecones to the summer tourists and how they'd use their dad's boat to fish and use the traps hanging in the trees to run a trapline this winter.

Not long after, headlights turned down the driveway. Everyone jumped. Cash whisper-yelled, "Get down! They'll see your heads through the window."

All the kids turtle-walked or belly-crawled to the back bedroom. Cash heard them scrambling and lifting each other out the window. Heard the soft thuds as their bodies hit the ground out back. She waited by the kitchen table until she heard a knock on the door. When she opened it, there stood the two federal agents who had been by the day she had driven up to talk with Josie.

They stood on the top stoop, the taller of the two

peering around and behind her trying to get a good look into the house.

"What can I do for you?" she asked.

"Are you the cousin that was here the other day?" one of the men asked.

"Yeah."

"What's your name?"

"Sarah."

"Sarah, you got a last name?"

"Day Dodge."

"We need to come in."

"Why?"

"We're investigating a man's death."

"He's dead. So's my cousin," said Cash.

"We need to talk to their children."

"They haven't come back from the wake yet."

"We were just there. Relatives said they didn't see them."

"Maybe they're walking home then."

"We need to come in." The one guy stepped forward. Cash backed up and walked to stand behind the couch that faced the picture window. The guy flipped on the light switch by the door. Both of them looked around and then walked to the kitchen table.

Damn, thought Cash.

"Looks like more than just you were eating."

Cash just looked at him. The other fed walked to the back bedrooms, poking his head into each room before entering. Cash could tell from the screech of bedsprings that he was leaning on the beds and looking under them, poking through the closets in each room.

When he reached the back bedroom, Cash heard the silence after he walked into the room and stood still. She could picture him staring at the open window. When he came back down the hallway, he walked right up to her.

"When did they leave?"

"About two hours ago, when their other aunt said the wake was starting at the community center."

"Two hours ago, huh? You don't say. Are you staying here?"

"Nah, I gotta get back home. Just wanted to go to the wake for one night."

"What do you mean one night? How many nights you all pray?"

"Four," answered Cash. "I came by to make sure the kids were all okay. Looks like they left a mess after eating, so I was just gonna clean up the supper stuff here and head into town myself."

She knew the whole situation wasn't making sense.

These same two guys had seen her once before in Halstad, and then up here the other day with Josie. You would think they would remember her and be more curious about how and why she was in both places. But if you went into Bemidji, all the Indians, dark-skinned and dark-haired, wore the same uniform—blue jeans, a T-shirt and long braids—men and women. Unless it was a soldier back from 'Nam, then his hair was short, growing out. To white folks, they looked alike.

She walked over to the kitchen table and started stacking plates and putting them in the sink. She ran some hot water and looked under the cupboard for some dish soap. She washed the plates, stacking them on a dishtowel on the counter. The two men stood by the picture window looking out, and then they went outside. Cash could hear them walking around the house, talking in low voices.

When the dishes were all washed, she wiped down the table and dried her hands on a shirt one of the kids had left draped over a kitchen chair. She pulled a twenty-dollar bill out of her jean pocket and stood thinking about where she could hide it so only Mary Jane would find it. Finally, she settled on the flour bag. Cash opened the bag and dropped the cash in. Folded the bag back over and set it down on the counter. The next time Mary Jane made frybread she would find it.

Cash put on the jean-jacket sweatshirt combo she had taken off to help cook.

She zipped up, checked the cigarette pack and saw there were only two left. *May as well leave them for the kids too*, she thought. She put them behind the flour bag, not trusting the feds. They might take them and smoke them themselves.

She took one more look around and left the house, pulling the inside door and the screen door shut tight behind her. The feds watched her drive away. Judging from the way they looked at her and started talking to each other, Cash wondered if maybe now they recognized her Ranchero. Too late. She was gone.

SHE DROVE ABOUT FIVE MILES, chain-smoking from the pack she had left lying on the car seat. She was looking for something. She almost passed it but then slowed, backed up and whipped the Ranchero down a hunting road. The truck bounced over ruts. A couple times Cash felt the hair on top of her head skim the roof of the truck. She kept going, jerking the wheel. She finally slammed on the brakes. Without turning off the headlights, she jumped out of the truck into a grove of maple trees.

"*Damn!*" she screamed at the top of her lungs. She thrashed along the hunting trail until she found a sizable branch. Putting both hands on it like she was swinging a baseball bat, she attacked the nearest tree, her braid down her back, swinging hard in the opposite direction. Screams, swear words and guttural sounds of rage echoed through the woods. When that first branch broke, Cash yelled, "Fuck you," and threw it as far as it would go, then stormed along the trail until she found another branch and kept raging on.

Bark flew in all directions. Unseen animals hurried to be even more unseen. *Fuck, fuck, fuck. Damn. Damn. Damn.* She screamed and attacked. When her physical strength gave out, she collapsed on the ground under a maple tree and sobbed deep gulping spasms of rage and grief. When that wave subsided, she wiped her nose and cheeks on the sleeve of her jean jacket.

She quieted. Now more gentle tears fell as she cried for the little girl who woke one day in jail and found herself alone for the next sixteen years. She cried for seven children who knew what they had lost, a mom and dad who loved them. She cried because those kids still had each other. And she cried for herself because she had no one. *Fuck. Damn.* Cash took another swipe at her eyes with the sleeve of her jacket.

Coming toward her was Josie Day Dodge. She was carrying a stack of birchbark winnowing baskets on her left hip. Her long black hair was swaying, hanging loosely down her back. Her hair curly, indicating it had recently been braided. Over her left shoulder hung strands of wiigwas.

As she passed Cash, she said, "Remember Eagle Straight Walker." And simultaneously with her words, a man danced himself into being, white eagle feather bustles were two circles on his back. As he danced, a shimmery white light emanated from him. As soon as he danced, he disappeared.

Josie turned halfway around and said, "The only job of big people is to protect the little people. You know, that drinking will kill you." And she walked deeper into the maple trees.

Cash watched her until she was out of sight. Another wave of grief and tears enveloped her. She lay on the ground, curled in a ball until the waves of grief subsided. The last time she wiped her face on her sleeve, she was even able to laugh a bit as she noticed how damp the sleeve was. "Oh shit," she said out loud as she jumped up and ran to her truck.

She slammed the light button in and killed the headlights. "Oh, please, dear god, Creator, please don't leave me stuck out here in the woods with Josie and the Eagle. Please, please," she begged as she turned the key in the ignition. "Thank you, thank you, thank you—a thousand migwetch'es," she breathed into the air as the truck engine turned over.

She sat there with her head resting on the steering wheel for a bit, then she made sure the truck was in neutral. She got back out and walked the maple grove, softly touching with her open palm each tree that she had struck with the branch. There was no *I'm sorry* or *Forgive me* in her touch, it was a touch of gratitude, a touch of love, a touch of *Here I am, I have left a part of me with you.*

She heard the trees sing a song to her, a song of sunshine. A song of healing. The trees, in the dark, danced the green and blues of the aurora borealis. Then Cash knew this time in the maple grove was done.

SHE WALKED TO THE TRUCK, put it in gear, and headed out to the main road. She hesitated a moment, then turned east toward Bemidji. When she hit town, she drove down Paul Bunyan Drive, past Paul and his big blue ox Babe. She turned again and crossed the railroad tracks until she saw the flashing neon Hamm's beer sign in a building that looked more like a deserted storefront than a bar.

When she parked, she could hear the jukebox, the lonely aching tempo of a country two-step drifting across the nighttime air. She figured she had about an hour to closing time. She checked her face in the rearview mirror. The tearstains were dried, the dirt from the woods wiped off. She smoothed her hair down, checked to make sure she had her smokes and got out of the truck. This close to closing time no one was going to care what she looked like anyways. The neon, the soft warmth of the dim lights, the boozy smoke smell—all beckoned. Calling her home.

She ordered a Bud right away, sliding her ID to the bartender without waiting to be asked, put some quarters up on the table and leaned against the wall closest to the pool table, drinking her beer. When her turn was up, she racked the balls and found a semi-straight stick.

She ran the table. Hoots and hollers rose up around the bar. "Oooh, we got us a shark."

"She's gonna take your money and run, Chuck."

"Rack 'em and weep."

Cash bent over the table, her bridge steady, the *crack* of the balls as she broke was a pleasing sound, almost as cool as the beer she was drinking. No balls dropped. When she walked back to the ledge where she had set her beer down, a black-haired, long-braids Indian guy, grinning, came and stood by her and said, "How's the curves, girl? Your place or mine?"

Cash laughed and walked back to the pool table to run the balls again, sinking the 8-ball by banking it back to the pocket on her left. As she stood waiting for the next sucker to pay and rack, Long Braids came and stood by her again. "We could be partners, you know." Grinning a grin that meant more than pool.

Cash said, "All righty, you break."

She turned to the guy who had just racked the balls. "Get yourself a partner and we'll play you last pocket."

She and her new partner held the table until closing time. The beer going down easy. The cigarettes burning long. When the bartender called last call, Long Braids went and got them each two more bottles. She finished one while they played the last game of pool, the second bottle she slipped under her arm inside her jean jacket.

Long Braids did the same with his, and they walked out of the bar with Long Braids' arm around her waist. When he started to steer her down the sidewalk, she led him to her truck. He whistled when he saw it and climbed in the passenger side.

Cash drove back the way she had come until she reached the railroad tracks.

Long Braids fiddled with the radio knob until he found a country station. Cash turned down a gravel street that ran along the railroad tracks and behind a grain elevator that set next to the tracks. She put the truck in park, with the ignition on so the radio kept playing. She lifted the beer bottle from between her thighs and took a drink. Long Braids took it from her, put it on the floor of the truck and pulled Cash over to his side of the truck. He put his hands on both sides of her head, just under her ears and kissed her. "Partners, aye?" he breathed.

The softness and tenderness of the lovemaking made silent tears run down Cash's cheeks. Long Braids didn't ask, didn't comment, just held her tighter and wiped the tears away with his thumbs. After a bit, after Cash's tears had run themselves dry, she pushed Long Braids up with her hands to his chest, pulled her shirt down and got her jeans up off the floor of the truck. She pulled them on still seated, lifting her pelvis just enough off the seat leather.

"You gonna tell me your name?" he asked.

"Cash. You?"

"J.R."

Cash cracked up laughing. "Every Indian guy I ever met is named Junior or Chuck."

"But I'm J.R."

"All righty, J.R. Long Braids."

"Long Braids?"

"Yeah, Long Braids."

He pulled her back for another kiss.

"I gotta go."

"Go? Where you gotta go to tonight?"

"Home."

"Whose home?" he asked, rubbing his thumb down her jawbone.

"Mine. Just mine. I gotta go." She slid behind the wheel, pushed the heat knob all the way to high. Soon a blast of warm air filled the truck.

"Where's home?"

"Fargo. Where you want me to drop you off?"

"I'm staying with my sister over here, about five blocks."

"You were going to take me to your sister's?" Cash laughed, backing the truck around.

"She wouldn't mind. Turn left up there at the feed store."

Cash drove him to a weathered house, a kid's trike sitting on the front lawn.

When Cash stopped the truck, he slid over and kissed her again, saying, "She really wouldn't mind."

"I gotta go."

"Fargo, aye?"

"Yep."

He kissed her one more time, slid over to the passenger side and hopped out. When he got to the top step, he turned and waved. Cash waved back and shifted into first.

SHE DROVE STRAIGHT THROUGH TO Fargo, arriving at her apartment just as the first rays of light were appearing on the east horizon. She was so tired she used the handrail to pull herself up the stairs. When she opened the screen door, a large envelope fell out. She picked it up and threw it on the kitchen table. Without turning on any lights, she stripped off her jeans and shoes and fell into bed.

When Cash woke up, she rolled over and grabbed the alarm clock, squinted to see the time. The numbers said it was eleven. She rolled back over and folded the pillow around her head. She lay still for a few moments before she peeked out again. She looked over at the window in her room. The shades were drawn, but she could tell it was dark. That didn't help her any. Why would it still be dark in the morning? She realized it must be night. *Damn*, she had slept the whole day.

She folded the pillow back around her head and sorted through the previous day—or would that be night? The Day Dodge kids, their parents dead, Long Braids, Josie warning her about drinking, Eagle Straight Walker. Her mind circled back to the Day Dodge kids and their dead parents. Cash wondered if Wheaton had figured out who had killed Tony O yet.

Damn, she had to pee. Cash crawled out of bed, her bare feet hitting the cold linoleum and sending chills up her body.

In the bathroom, she remembered the envelope that had been between the screen door and wooden door of her apartment. She walked out and picked it up. She took it back to bed with her, turned on the lamp and opened it. There was a typewritten note that said, "Sign and go."

She looked at the rest of the papers. They were papers from the White Earth Chippewa Tribe's education office. Everything had been filled out, typewritten, in her legal name—Renee Blackbear—with her legal age. Nineteen. Another set of papers, also filled out by typewriter, were enrollment papers for Moorhead State College. Cash didn't even know how to process the information. She stuffed the whole bunch under her pillow and fell back asleep.

HER SLEEP THIS TIME WAS restless, Tony O and Josie wandering in and out of her dreams, the kids walking through woods, Eagle's dancing and cheerleaders at a football game, the stands filled with folks standing and yelling, then back to Josie walking through the maple trees.

When Cash woke up a second time, she could see pale light between the crack of the window shade. It must really be morning this time. She reached over to the dresser to get the alarm clock, but it wasn't there. She remembered pulling it to the bed earlier and, sure enough, there it was under her pillow along with the papers she had looked at the night before. It was 7:00 A.M.

Cash reached over the bed to the floor and sifted through the clothes until she found a pair of socks. She pulled them on and walked to the bathroom to run hot water in the tub. She caught a glimpse of herself in the mirror. Lord, did she look rugged. Eyes puffy from crying, drinking and smoking. Her hair sticking out in all directions, scraggly loops that had come loose from the braid.

She brushed her teeth and felt a little more human. She made sure the door in the kitchen was locked, then went back and crawled into the tub.

Who in the heck had left those papers? Filled them out? And who in hell thought she should go to college? Cash didn't know that many people. Or, maybe she knew a lot of people, but most of the folks she knew were farm laborers. None of them would have gone to all that trouble. Not any of the guys from the bars she frequented.

Wheaton. That would have to be her best guess, 'cause Jim would never think of something like Cash going to college. Cash lay in the tub until the water turned lukewarm then drained half the water out and filled it with more hot water.

College. *What the heck did folks do at college?* Cash didn't even know anyone who had ever gone to college. Back when she was going to school, a couple of the white kids, the valedictorian and salutatorian who had each given a speech on graduation night, they had gone on to college. But the rest of the farm kids were going to work their daddy's farm until Daddy died and passed it on to them. The girls were going to marry a farmer, probably the same farm kid they had gone steady with all through high school. In fact, sometimes in Piggly Wiggly, she would run into some of the girls she went to school with. They would have a baby on a hip and sometimes a toddler running alongside them. Cash never knew what to say. Mostly she would just say a quiet *hi* and keep walking. The mothers had carts that they were filling with groceries, feeding the farm hands on their daddy-in-law's farms, while Cash walked through the store with her meager purchases tucked under an arm. Maybe a pound of hamburger, for sure eggs and a couple cans of Campbell's tomato soup, a loaf of bread. A can of Folgers. More often than not the hamburger spoiled before Cash got around to frying it up.

All this thinking about food and shopping made Cash realize the water had once again turned cold and that she was starving. She stood up, grabbed a towel off the rack, quick-dried herself and wrapped the towel around her before going to look in the fridge.

There was nothing inside except a couple eggs in a carton and some beers. As she stood with the fridge door open, she remembered different foster homes. Those fridges were always filled with food. Cheese, eggs, orange juice, yesterday's beef stew, canned peaches, Tupperware containers full of the weekly leftovers. All of it off-limits to her.

She had compared notes one time at school with another foster girl who was from Leech Lake. If she remembered right, her name was Sue Fox. Maybe Jane Fox. Anyways, the other girl had talked about the full fridge at her foster home and how she wasn't allowed to just go in and take something, not even the leftovers. Cash had said, "I can't either. But sometimes I sneak frozen cookies from the freezer late at night. If I get caught, you'll know by the whip marks on my legs. Or maybe I'll be wearing tights for two weeks straight to cover the marks." Both girls had laughed and agreed their foster parents were evil.

Cash shut the fridge door. She needed food. She walked back into the bathroom and scooped up the clothes she had dropped on the floor. She did the same with the four piles of jeans, undies and socks that circled her bed. Someday she would have to learn to be a little neater.

She dumped the clothes on top of the other dirty clothes in a pile in the corner of the room. She got a fresh set of clothes off the overstuffed chair and clean underwear and socks from the dresser. Unbraided her hair and went back to the kitchen sink to wash it. Too lazy to run a brush or comb through her damp hair, she just twisted it into a bun on top of her head, held in place by a yellow pencil shoved through it.

She stuffed all her laundry into a canvas laundry bag, grabbed a handful of quarters from her top dresser drawer. She put on her jean jacket. It had dirt on the arms and back, either from when the kids had dragged her through the woods or when she had attacked the maples. Either way, it too needed to be washed. She stuffed it in the laundry bag and put on a sweatshirt over her T-shirt. Her tennis shoes were filthy too, so those got stuffed on top of the jean jacket and she put on her cowboy boots.

She pulled the door shut behind her, locked up and walked to the Lost Sock at the end of the block. Only two of the twelve washers were filled. A lone man reading the *Fargo Forum* was the only other customer.

Cash dumped her clothes into two machines, not bothering to sort coloreds from whites, jeans from lighter cottons. In Cash's mind, if they couldn't all be washed together she didn't have any use for them.

Cash went to the little vending machine on the wall that reminded her of the machines in women's restrooms, but this vending machine gave you laundry soap and bleach, not feminine products. She bought one tiny box of Tide, dumped half in one washer, half in the other, slid her quarters in and waited until she heard the water running into the machine.

Once she knew the machines worked—not always so at the Lost Sock—she walked back to her truck and headed to Shari's Kitchen. There she sat on a stool at the counter and ordered eggs, pancakes, toast and bacon. She ate without thinking, left a five on the counter when she was finished and drove back to her apartment, then walked to the Lost Sock. The whole drive and eating had taken her less than forty-five minutes.

The lone man was gone from the laundromat. She corralled a wire cart on wheels and loaded the wet clothes into it, sorting the clothes into jeans and cotton. The jeans would take two coins and the cottons just one.

She sat down to read the *Fargo Forum* back to

front, funnies first, while her clothes dried. Drying clothes wouldn't give her enough time to read the whole paper, so she figured to get the good news first. When the first dryer stopped, she stood up, filled the wire cart with the warm clothes. She held an armful to her chest before putting them into the cart. Ah, that this kind of warmth would always be present. But even as she held the clothes to her, they cooled off. She dumped them in the cart and wheeled them over to the folding counter. By the time she had neat stacks of folded T-shirts, socks, undies and bedsheets, her jeans and towels were dry, which she folded as well. Done, Cash stuffed everything back into the canvas bag, except the jeans, and took it all home to her apartment.

She put everything away. Swept the floors of her small apartment, opened the window shades in the living room/ bedroom and put the clock back up on the dresser, just so, so she could read it from bed without getting up.

There were no mementos on the dresser top. No family photos. No jewelry box. There was, however, a half-empty box of .22 shells. She kept it just like Wheaton kept his place in Ada. Sparse. No photos or mementos either. There had been a box of shotgun shells sitting on his kitchen counter though. At least she had a couple pool trophies won in some tournament or other.

And some blue chalk. Cash had a habit of pocketing the chalk that bars set on the edge of the tables for the players. There were nine pieces of chalk on her dresser. She'd have to try and remember to take a few back to the Casbah.

She opened the top drawer of the dresser and counted the quarters. Fifteen dollars' worth, which she dropped into a lone sock that she then knotted at the opening. Farther back in the drawer was what was left of her bankroll from the season's work. She had enough for rent, which was coming up, and a couple twenties. If she caught Jim early enough at the Casbah, maybe she could talk him into going over to the Flame this weekend where they were having a winner-take-all pool tournament. The Flame was a strip joint and it was fairly easy to rake in a bunch of money as the only girl playing on the tables. The men's attention was definitely not focused on their game, but Cash liked to have Jim with, even though she would have to split the take, because sometimes the men got a little too grabby.

There: laundry done, belly fed, money counted and a plan made to get some more money. Cash couldn't avoid it any longer. She picked up her pillow and gathered the papers she had stuffed under there. She went out to her little kitchen and discovered one more diversion. Cash made a pot of coffee and once done, poured it into her thick white ceramic cup. She sat down at the table and read the papers, word for word, line for line.

She saw now that her high school report cards were included. Whoever had typed the papers had put little red ink X's on the signature lines where her name would go. Cash pictured the campus that she drove by when she went to Shari's Kitchen. A wooded campus with a thick winding sidewalk visible from the road. College kids wearing jeans, longhaired, books tucked under arms. Right now, the college was empty, according to the papers in front of her. The actual fall term would start in a week and a half.

Cash smoked and drank her coffee. Filled her cup when that one was empty and lit another cigarette. She had always liked school. School had been a refuge from the foster homes. In grade school she had been a bit of a bully. She had learned early that when she started a new school, if she fought the toughest kid the first chance she got, after that everyone tended to leave her alone. And when she started working the fields, she ended up working with a lot of her male peers over the summer so going to school with them was easy. The teachers tended to like her because she liked learning. Liked reading. Even with her drinking weekends all through high school, she had been a straight-A student. But not once had anyone ever said to her, "Why don't you go to college?" And here, sitting in front of her, was her opportunity. Cash signed her name next to the various red X's just to see what it felt like.

The more she thought about it, the more she was sure it had to have been Wheaton who had dropped these off. He had signed as her guardian after she had gotten this apartment and still had a year and a half of high school to finish. That was the one condition Wheaton had placed on her. That she finish school— and she had. She lit another cigarette and filled her coffee cup for the third time. She sat back down and looked out the window to Main Avenue.

She could see the front end of her blue Ranchero. She leaned forward enough to see the edge of the Casbah sign. She heard a train rumble by on the tracks a couple blocks from her apartment, heard an appliance truck, engine running, sitting in the alleyway.

This was her world, a living breathing country western song—a truck, a bar, a train and a back alley.

College?

What day was it? She had been in so many different places, over such short amounts of time, with a lot of beer thrown in there for good measure, she had to stop and try to recollect what day it actually was. Then she remembered she had read the *Forum* down in the laundromat. She had a trick with her memory, where she would pull up a page she had read and could visualize it in her mind. She did this now with the *Fargo Forum*. She pulled up the funnies because she had spent the most time reading that page, and yep, there in the upper right-hand corner was today's date: Monday, August 24, 1970.

Damn, she was missing a day of work. But it was Monday. Cash figured a college would be open on a Monday.

She stuffed the signed papers back into the envelope, stuck her cigarettes into the front pocket of her clean jean jacket, went downstairs and fired up the truck. She traced her way back toward Shari's Kitchen until she reached the Moorhead State campus, where she parked on the street across from the main archway that led to the campus proper.

She pulled a cigarette out, rolled down the truck window and lit up.

She sat there smoking, looking at the world around her. There was so much more green here than around her apartment.

On the other side of the street was a flat modern building that called itself the MSC Lutheran Students' Association. There weren't any students around but Cash saw a couple teacher-types walking across the grass between the red brick buildings.

There was a wooden sign that said Administration Building, with a gold-toned arrow pointing at the closest red-brick building. If she was going to do this, she better do it. She flicked the cigarette out onto the pavement and grabbed the envelope from the seat beside her. She had to wait for a break in traffic and then ran across the street, not bothering to walk to the corner and cross.

Cash felt a queasiness in her stomach, the same feeling she would sometimes get bent over the pool table, lining up a shot at the 8-ball, with either a tournament trophy or something like fifty bucks riding on her making the shot. Cash slowed her walk as she got closer to the entrance of the Administration Building.

She pulled open the door and was surprised at how dark the inside seemed. Quiet and dark. The only sound was her footsteps walking across the smooth brick floor. She stopped for a moment and looked around, taking in her surroundings. There was a window that looked like a bank window, with the screen rolled down: Not open for business. There were other windows where Cash could see women sitting behind desks, typing. There was a sign on a door that said Administrative Offices. Cash knocked.

"Come in."

She opened the door and poked her head in. "I'm wondering where I turn papers in to register for school," she mumbled.

"'Cuse me?" asked the woman.

Cash cleared her throat, raising her voice a little. "I'm wondering where I turn papers in to register for school."

"Oh!" said the woman, "that would be right across the way there." She pointed in the direction behind Cash. "Right over there where it says Registrar's Office. Take your papers right over there. Cindy will help you. She's the one working today. You're a little late with those, so you better make sure you get them in."

"Thanks," said Cash, shutting the door behind her.

184 · MARCIE R. RENDON

She felt the woman watch her as she walked across the hall and knocked on the door that read Registrar's Office.

Cindy was a lot older than her name implied. Cash expected women whose names ended with *y* to be cheerleader-types, perky and young. This Cindy was wearing orthopedic shoes with eyeglasses hanging on a beaded string around her neck, with a different pair of glasses set toward the front of her nose. Her hair was overpermed and she wore a dress like Cash had only seen farm wives wear to church on Sunday.

"How can I help you?" she asked Cash.

"I want to register for school."

"You need to fill out the paperwork," said Cindy. "Let me get those for you."

"I already have them."

"Oh. Well, let me see."

Cindy took off the glasses perched on her nose and put on the ones hanging around her neck. "Hmmmm. Well, these are all in order. You never took any SATs?"

Cash didn't know what Cindy was talking about. "No."

"Well, we have a minority waiver on the tests. You can start your freshman year, but you have to take them before the end of the school year. Think you can do that?"

"Yes."

"And the Minnesota Chippewa Tribe will give you a full scholarship, I see. So, really, all you need to do is fill out these papers to get yourself a dorm room." Cindy reached back to a metal file cabinet and pulled out some sheets of paper that were stapled together, then handed them to Cash.

"What did you say?" asked Cash.

"These are the papers you need to fill out to stay in the dorm."

Cash held the papers out to Cindy. "I'll be staying in my own apartment."

Cindy switched glasses and peered at Cash. "Honey, freshman girls are NOT allowed to live off campus. All our girls stay on campus."

"I'll stay in my own apartment," Cash repeated.

"No, honey, it's not allowed."

Cash reached over to pick up the registration papers and turned to walk out. "Of course, some girls who live with their families, they don't have to live on campus," Cindy said.

"So if I live with my family, I don't have to live in a dorm?" Cash asked without turning around.

"That's right, honey. Of course, we need these signed and a letter from your parents saying that you are living with them."

Cash turned and set the registration papers back on Cindy's desk and stood there without saying anything.

"Well," said Cindy. "You bring me that letter and come back on Wednesday."

"Wednesday?"

"Wednesday is when everyone registers for their classes if they didn't pre-register. Which you didn't. So you need to come in on Wednesday and get your classes. There will be a line of students outside that window"—she pointed to what Cash had thought of as a bank window. "That's where you line up to get your classes. Bright and early, eight in the morning."

"All right." Cash turned and left. *Damn!* she thought as she walked across the green lawn. *Damn.*

She made a U-turn when there was a break in cars and headed straight to Ada. She stormed into the jail and slapped the parental consent forms to live off campus in front of Wheaton. He picked up the papers and burst out laughing when he read them.

"You think this is funny!" Cash yelled at him. "I made a fool of myself going to that college and turning those papers in. You know I can't live on campus! In a dorm with a bunch of white girls! Wheaton, I'll end up killing someone. I can't do this. I can't live with a bunch of white girls."

"Slow down, Cash. Slow down."

"Why did you do this?" Cash's eyes filled with tears.

"Ah, girl, I didn't know about any rule that you had to live on campus. You're too smart to drive grain truck the rest of your life. Or beet truck. You could be a lawyer. You could be a teacher."

Cash rolled her eyes.

"Well, maybe not. You could teach girls Phys Ed. Heck, I don't know, Cash, I just know you can do more than what you're doing. And the Tribe will pay for you to go to college. I thought what the hell, it's worth a try. You'll go, won't you?"

"I can't live in a dorm, Wheaton."

"Well, I signed for that apartment you're in. We'll just fudge a bit and say that you live there with your guardian."

"You'd do that?"

Wheaton didn't answer. He just signed the papers Cindy had given her. Then he rolled his chair around to face the typewriter. *Click. Click. Click.* Cash smoked a cigarette while Wheaton typed. He stopped typing and rolled the paper out of the typewriter and signed it with an ink pen. "There you go, girl. Take these back and turn them into whoever you need to turn them into. I think you need to get a phone too."

"A phone?"

"Yeah, a phone. Going to college, you'll need a phone. You'll need to go to classes. You won't be able to run back and forth like you been doing. If you have a phone, we could talk by phone. How was the trip up to Red Lake? See, if you had a phone, I could call you and you tell me, not have to drive all the way up here."

"A phone?"

"Take it you haven't watched the news either. Some folks have a TV these days. Or a radio that works, in their house, not just in their truck."

Cash blew smoke in his direction. "I do have a radio."

He waved the smoke away with his big hand. "We have another dead body."

Cash sat up. "Where? Who?"

"This one's a white guy."

Cash sat back and took another drag of her cigarette and waited for Wheaton to continue.

"He was found in that big ditch north of town. About half a mile from where Tony O's body was dumped."

"Shot?"

"Nope, this one was choked to death looks like. Looks like they—whoever *they* are—were parked up along that road drinking. Lots of beer bottles and cigarette butts thrown out around there. The body is already down in the basement of the county hospital. Thought we could drive over there. Figured you'd be out this way today, so I was just kind of hanging around waiting for you to show up."

Cash was tempted to swear at him again. Instead she stood up. "Let's go then."

They climbed into Wheaton's cruiser and headed to the county hospital.

On the drive, Cash asked, "How come you don't have any pictures of your family in your house?"

Wheaton ignored her.

"At least I got pool trophies," Cash said.

No answer.

At the hospital they entered the back door and headed downstairs. There was no one there today. When Wheaton went to ring the buzzer for the doc, Cash stopped his hand and just walked in. Wheaton followed her. Cash went to the walk-in freezer and opened the door.

There was only one body in there. She headed toward the end of the metal table where the white sheet covered a rounded lump and pulled the sheet down. A dusky pallor covered the young man's face. His neck had black and blue marks where hands or a rope had circled it. She covered the man's face and made her way out of the freezer, Wheaton still following behind.

Out of the room, she stood looking up out the basement window. A strip of grass waved in the breeze and she could see bits of blue sky. *Healing rays of god's love, wash gently over me.* The guy was just a kid. Not much older than she was. She turned to Wheaton and said, "I remember his name. When he came into Arnie's, one of the guys called him John. They seemed to know who he was with."

"I asked around," Wheaton said. "There was a whole group of men that came over from the Dakotas, most of them young."

"Yeah, they were in the bar that night."

"Apparently they hightailed it out of town. Three of them left without picking up their checks. One of the men who didn't pick up his check was named John

Swenson. Figure that's him lying in there. The other two, I had my clerk call them when she came in for a few hours. They just went home for the weekend and are driving back into the Valley today. They don't sound like our guys. And besides, John here was killed last night. Figure that means our two outlaws are still around."

"Who all have you talked to?" Cash asked.

"All the men I can find. Been up and down the Valley. Out to all the big farms that hire on. No one's heard anything or seen anything suspicious."

"Which farm were the Dakota boys working?"

"Wang's."

"Well, when John came into Arnie's, he walked over and talked to the Dakota boys. They have to know something."

"Maybe so," said Wheaton, "but they're not talking to me. Heard one of them was running the table at Mickey's last night."

"Thanks a lot, Wheaton. Now I'm catfish bait?"

"I'm just saying . . ."

"Yeah, I know. I have to be back in Fargo by eight Wednesday morning to register for classes. Seems I'll be registering late," Cash said pointedly.

"Come on back to the jail and you can read over

my interview notes from the guys I talked to. Maybe you'll see something I didn't."

"S'pose I could. Was thinking of driving out to Wang's myself and signing on for sugar beet harvest."

"You're going to school."

"I could work graveyard shift," answered Cash. "There's a tournament at the Flame this coming weekend. Figured I would go to that, make enough money to last a couple of weeks."

"Those papers said you get a full scholarship to go to school. Including living expenses."

"Yeah, but I just turned them all in today. I think I actually have to start school before they hand me over any money."

Wheaton laughed as they headed outside.

She slid inside his cruiser and pushed in the cigarette lighter. "Wonder where old Felix is?"

"Maybe he actually had some doctoring to do."

When they got back to the jail, the clerk Diane was in. Cash said hi and sat down on a chair by the main desk to be closer to the ashtray. Wheaton gave her a handful of sheets of lined paper with his notes. Cash read and smoked. The notes didn't tell her much more than what she already knew—or didn't know—except for the fact that the Wang farm appeared to be where the guys involved worked.

After about a half hour of reading, she stood up, stretched and said, "I think I should drive out to Wang's and see about a job."

"Let's go get a bite to eat at the Drive-Inn first," Wheaton suggested, pushing back from his desk in the other room. He had been sitting in there with his door open while Cash was reading. "I'll buy. When's the last time you ate?"

"Went to Shari's Kitchen. Last night or the night before."

"Well, come on, let me get you a hamburger."

Wheaton drove the seventeen miles from Ada to Halstad so they could eat at the Drive-Inn, the only place to get a decent hamburger in the county. They pulled into one of the slots and waited for the waitress to come out and take their order. Wheaton rolled down his window when she came back with two burgers and fries in baskets on a metal tray that hooked over the door through the open window. They ate in silence, one or the other occasionally making a comment about the weather. When did Wheaton think beet harvest would start? And these had to be the best french fries in the Valley.

WHEN THEY WERE DONE EATING, Wheaton drove
Cash back to her Ranchero. "Take care," Wheaton
said.

Cash headed west of town to the Wang farmstead.
It was a warm August day. Interestingly, it wasn't as
humid this close to Ada as it was just seventeen miles
closer to the river. The air smelled of harvest. Wheat,
oats, some late alfalfa. The short growing season this
far north meant that some fields were already plowed
under. As she drove past the Johnson farm, someone
was spreading cow manure on an eighty-acre square.
It added a whole new smell to the air.

Cash could see the Wang farm up ahead. Everything
about the farmstead said prosperity. The barn and
outbuildings were painted a shiny white. The three-
story farmhouse, though older, was painted the same
white, making it look stately as opposed to just old.
A quarter-acre vegetable garden was laid out behind
the house.

Cash could see asparagus gone to fern and the
season's left-over rows of sweet corn. A couple of
kids' bikes lay on the front lawn. Cash drove down
the gravel driveway, past the house, and parked at the
outbuilding that served as Milt Wang's office.

She got out of the truck and walked up to the door,

pulling the screen open and walking in. There was a desk piled with papers and a black rotary phone sitting on it. The floor was linoleum and there was an electric fan running, sitting slightly off-center from the doorway, pulling some breeze in. It all spoke of money, lending credence to the statement that the Red River Valley was the breadbasket of the world.

Cash heard the screen door open behind her. She turned as Milt walked in. He was a short stocky man, with a mustache that reminded Cash of one of the Three Stooges.

"Cash!" he exclaimed, holding out his right hand to shake hers. "You here to sign up for beet harvest?"

Cash shook his hand. Unlike most farmers' calloused work hands, his hand was smooth like a banker's. Cash had to restrain herself from shaking with the eerie goose bumps that ran through her body at his touch. He was dressed like a farmer: work jeans, plaid shirt, Red Wing boots, but everything was just a little too new, a little too unworked in. Cash suspected he had been sitting in his house, probably watching some afternoon TV with his wife and had come out when he saw her truck pull up.

"Thought I'd see if you could use anyone on the graveyard shift," Cash said.

"That I always need," Milt said. "I don't know about hiring on a girl though. Nighttimes get a little rough."

"I can handle myself."

"I would hate to have something happen." The look in his eyes belied his overly sincere tone.

"I can deal with it. It'll keep me out of the bars and off the pool table," Cash said. "Besides, seems like your hired hands have had a bit more trouble lately than any I've ever had as a girl working here in the fields."

"It's a shame, isn't it? You got a point there all right," said Milt. "First that Indian from up at Red Lake and now that young boy from the Dakotas. Hope to heck Wheaton, or those feds that been coming around, find out who's behind this craziness. Speaking of which, a young woman like you, even if you are an Indian, shouldn't be hanging out in bars all the time like you do. Driving all over by yourself alone in that truck of yours. Folks talk, you know."

"Well, if you hire me, they'll have a little less to talk about for a while." Cash smiled, while in her head she wanted to kick him in the balls the way the Day Dodge kid had kicked her ankle.

"Got a point there."

"When do you think you'll start up?" asked Cash.

"Few weeks at least. How'll I get a hold of you?"

"You can just leave word with Wheaton. I'd have to drive one of your trucks, you know."

"We can work that out. Just show up a bit early each night to gas up."

"All right." Cash started to leave. At the door she turned and said, "So both those men worked for you?"

"Yes, they did. A lot of praying the wife and I have been doing. Hoping that this mess gets cleaned up soon. Don't need this kind of trouble hanging over our place here."

"You think I need to watch out for anyone in particular?" Cash asked.

"Now, girl, I really don't think it is any of the men I hired on. Probably some drifter, going through on the train or maybe one of them migrants stayed behind and is rolling men instead of working a decent day's work."

"Okay, just thought I'd ask."

She sat for a minute in her truck. She could see Milt watching her from behind the screen door. She backed around and drove out to the main road. In the rearview mirror, she saw him walk to his house. She turned and headed toward Ada. *What the hell?* It was a big county when you thought about it. There were probably fifty small towns that the men could go drink in, with as many drugstore counters for them to get a quick meal at. Cash pulled over to the side of the road. Quieted her mind. Lost herself in the white clouds drifting overhead and the soft breeze that floated over the wheat fields still standing, shimmering in the afternoon sun. She lost track of time, lost track of her thoughts.

A grain truck rumbling toward her, dust billowing up behind it, brought her out of her reverie. All her instincts told her to keep driving, drive straight out of the county and keep going. But as the truck driver passed, she raised a hand in a wave, as was the custom here in farm country. Everyone was a neighbor, at least in church speak. They would gossip and lie and sleep with each other's wives—and apparently kill each other—but neighborliness was the standard they measured themselves against.

She had some time before it made sense to show up in the bars over in Halstad, so she stopped at the Woolworth's Five and Dime in Ada and bought shampoo and hand soap. The way the two store clerks watched her got on her nerves. Keeping their eyes on an Indian woman when it should be those blond Sorenson kids they should be watching. When she went up to the register to pay, the two clerks talked to each other as if she weren't there, all the while ringing up her purchases and taking her money, dropping her change into her hand without touching her skin. Cash looked at the clerk and asked, "Is that a spider crawling on your shoulder?"

The woman frantically started brushing away at her shoulder, asking the other woman, "Where is it? Get it off me."

Cash walked out smiling.

Cash left Ada and drove west toward Halstad. The flat river plain was broken only by clumps of trees that marked farmsteads, the wavy line of trees in front of her marking the Red River's meandering path north. In her rearview mirror, the highway was a straight ribbon going back toward Ada.

She got into Halstad way too early to go to either bar, so she stopped at the Drive-Inn and had a repeat of the lunch she and Wheaton had had earlier. There was still a lot of time before the men started leaving the fields and coming into the bars. Cash went to Lucky's Fuel and waited while some high school kid, too small to be out on the football field, put fuel in the truck, checked the oil and washed her windshields. Cash thanked him and drove north out of town.

In a mile she reached the road that ran east and west along the big ditch, the ditch where the young man had been killed. *Had been forced to quit living*, she thought. She turned down the road and pulled over at the spot where Wheaton's notes had indicated the murder happened. She walked down into the ditch where the grass had been trampled, both by the body, which had lain there, and then the various folks who had come by to deal with the body, Wheaton being one of them.

Cash couldn't really get a feel or a picture of what had happened. All she felt was an all-encompassing wave of sadness. She wondered who the young man's family was, would they grieve the same way Josie did? And now how Josie's children grieved her.

Cash had been alone for so long, she didn't quite grasp what she supposed were normal feelings when you loved someone, when you cared for someone. She *would* feel bad if something happened to Wheaton. Yeah, that's true.

She heard tires on gravel coming down the road and walked up out of the ditch.

Coming down the road was a dark blue pickup truck. Two men in it. The driver slammed on the brakes so that Cash was eye level with his elbow pointing out the truck window. Their truck was between Cash and her truck. There was a nagging feeling in Cash's gut that made her wish this wasn't true.

"What you doin' this far off the reservation?" the driver wanted to know.

Cash looked at him. He was wearing a blue work shirt, rolled up just past his elbows. Where the collar of his shirt was open, his throat was sunburnt red. His short hair, combed straight back, wasn't quite blond. Standing as she was at the edge of the road, still on the ditch slope, she couldn't see the second man.

"I drive truck, same as most folks around here," Cash said.

"That so? Doesn't look like you're working too hard today."

Cash lied. "I come out along this ditch and set gopher traps. This here is Milt Wang's field and he pays me thirty-nine cents for each pair of gopher feet I bring him."

The guy turned to the other man sitting in the truck. "Did you hear that? Indians have gone from trapping beaver to trapping gophers. And they got little girls doing it now. The men are all big chiefs, driving grain truck and all. Well, well."

Turning to face Cash out the window, he said, "You better be careful. We heard there was a dead injun just about a quarter of a mile over and then one of the boys from the Dakotas ended up in the ditch just a bit from where you're standing. That long hair of yours might just get caught in one of your traps. It would be a shame to have all that hair wrapped around your neck and no way for you to get out. And far enough out of town so that no one would hear you scream."

Both men started laughing.

Cash stepped up on the gravel and started to walk behind their truck to get to hers.

They were right. No one in town would hear her if they decided to be crazy.

More laughter. "Aw, we didn't mean to scare you. Come on back and talk to us."

Cash walked around the back end of their pickup and over to the passenger side of her Ranchero. She wasn't going to get trapped between the two trucks, that was for damn sure.

She crawled in on the passenger side, digging her

keys out of her pocket as she got in. She put the keys in the ignition, clutch and brake in, shifted into reverse, eased up on both pedals and backed around the end of their truck. She turned the wheel a hard left, threw the gears into first and took off, rapidly shifting into second, third and fourth. When the dust settled behind her, she saw that they were still sitting in their truck on the road where she had left them.

She downshifted. Without stopping, she took the corner that led her back into town. When she got there, she turned over her right shoulder and looked back. With flat field all the way across, she could see their truck still sitting there.

Huh, she thought. She wondered if anyone saw anything the night before. There was a block of houses on the north side of town. Bedroom windows faced the open field. She drove down the block, made a U-turn and cruised back.

A group of girls, somewhere between the ages of eleven and fourteen, came running around the corner of one of the houses. They were town girls. Wearing plaid shorts and white sleeveless blouses. Cash guessed they were probably the future cheerleaders of the town. Cash pulled over and got out.

"Hey, Kathy," she hollered to the one girl whose

name she knew. The group stopped, saw it was Cash and stood, some of them leaning hands on thighs, catching their breath.

Kathy waved at Cash and said something to her friends that Cash couldn't make out. Cash had been working the fields for so many years that as the only young Indian woman doing so, everyone seemed to know who she was, even if she didn't know them. But she knew Kathy because she often sat behind the counter in the bakery in town while her mother worked the cash register. They shared a love of jelly-filled bismarcks.

"Hi, Cash," she said. "What are you doing in town?"

"Thought I'd shoot a few games of pool tonight. Maybe swing a partner or two around on Arnie's new dance floor."

The kids laughed and poked each other. Shooting pool and dancing were exotic activities for town kids whose lives revolved around Vacation Bible School in the summer and the high school football and basketball teams once school started.

Cash went and walked behind the house the kids had come running around. They followed her like ducklings chasing their mother. Cash stood looking at the truck sitting a mile away on the gravel road. One of the kids said, "Hey, that's where they found that guy's body. Someone killed him, choked him like wringing a chicken's neck is what my dad said."

"And they killed that Indian guy right over there," chimed in another kid, pointing a little more northwest than where the truck sat.

"Do you think those are the killers, back to make sure they didn't leave any clues?" *From the mouths of babes*, thought Cash as a cold chill ran from the base of her spine to the edge of her back hairline. The thought had never occurred to her minutes ago when those two had driven up on her.

"Look, they're leaving," one of the younger girls said, pointing.

A bigger girl grabbed her arm and pushed it down, saying, "Knock it off, you want them to know we saw them? I'm getting out of here." She took off around the building with the flock of kids following her. Cash watched the truck turn north at the crossroads and then she went to find the kids.

They were sitting on Kathy's front porch when she rounded the corner, chatting excitedly about were they brave enough to walk over to the ditch, see if there were any clues. Some of the girls wanted to stay back, *'cause it was a man's job*. Some of the girls said the others could go if they wanted to. Cash leaned against the step railing and asked, "Is that the first time you all saw that truck over there?"

One little girl said, "There were all kinds of cars and trucks and the sheriff's car over there when they found the body."

"Our mom wouldn't let us go look. She told us to go inside and watch TV, like it was Saturday or something. There are no cartoons on during the week."

"The night before last, Susan slept over," Kathy said, "and we climbed out our bedroom window and were laying in the grass behind the house. We saw a car or truck over there, didn't we?" she asked, turning to a young girl who wore plaid shorts and a cotton blouse that matched.

"Yeah," said Susan. "We thought it was high school kids. Sometimes they go over there to . . . you know . . ." The girls giggled. "But we could hear men's voices. At one point they were yelling at each other."

"But we couldn't hear what they were saying."

"Do you think it was a truck like the one that was just out there?" asked Cash, although she was pretty certain of the answer even if they weren't.

"I don't know," said Kathy. "About that time my

dad came home and he went into my room to say goodnight to me and we got caught out here. He hollered at us to get our butts back in the house."

"They were still parked out there at around midnight," Kathy remembered, "'cause we snuck out to the kitchen to get some of her mom's brownies and when we were looking out the kitchen window, we saw their taillights go off and on a couple times."

"Well, kids, you better listen to your parents and stay close to home until Wheaton gets this straightened out. Your parents would be bawling for a year and a day if something happened to one of you."

"Not mine," piped up the one little girl. "My dad said that next year at the county fair he's gonna send me off to live with the carnies. He's had enough of me, he says."

"Me too!"

"Yeah, you look like a circus kid."

A series of friendly taunts. The younger kids were once again chasing each other around the yard. Cash waved at Kathy and walked back to her truck. She sat in the warm August air, lit a cigarette and recalled the ice that had crept up her back when the kid had said, "Maybe they were back making sure they hadn't left any clues." She shivered with the thought.

She flicked the cigarette out into the street, started up the truck and drove to Mickey's. She ordered a Coke and played herself at the pool table. She and the bartender chatted back and forth about the weather, crops, Bucky cheating on his wife, the price of wheat down on the Grain Exchange . . . he behind the bar smoking and reading the *Fargo Forum*, she practicing her bank shots.

At dusk the farmers started to drift in, shaking the chaff out of their duckbill hats and bringing in the smell of field dust with them. Quarters were dropped in the jukebox, country twang mixed in with the Minnesota Scandinavian brogue.

Cash toned down her game, won some, lost some. She was drinking slow, waiting for the right time to mosey across the street to Arnie's. She figured if the two men came back into town, they would go on over there to drink. She planned to hang around until they showed again, trusting the cold chill that ran up her back and the young kids' intuition about cleaning up clues left behind.

WHEN THE TEN O'CLOCK NEWS came on, Cash watched while the body bags were counted and the protest marches covered, then she went out the side door of Mickey's to grab the extra pack of cigarettes she'd thrown in the glove box earlier in the day when she had stopped for gas.

She heard an engine running and when she looked down the block to see who it was, she heard footsteps coming up behind her. Before she could turn around, her arms were grabbed from behind, elbows pulled together, and a rope quickly wrapped around her wrists before a gunnysack reaching almost to her knees was pulled over her head. The dank smell of potatoes gagged her as she was swung headfirst over a man's shoulders. Then she was dumped in the bed of a pickup truck that had its engine running.

The passenger side door slammed shut and the pickup jerked back out of its parking spot and whipped around the corner. Cash rolled and crashed into one side of the pickup bed and then the other.

When the truck made another sharp right turn and the road turned to gravel, Cash knew in her mind where she was going. These guys were bound and determined to clean up loose ends, get rid of all clues. Somehow they knew she was one of the clues and she still didn't know these jokers' names.

Cash spit burlap fiber out of her mouth. She was

trying to breathe through her mouth because the foul smell of rotten potatoes kept gagging her, but every time she opened her mouth she inhaled field dust or burlap fiber.

The pickup slowed and took another turn, this time to the left onto a dirt road. Cash could hear the grass that grew in the middle of the tire tracks scrape against the undercarriage. About right now they were driving past the spot where they had dumped Tony O's body. Up ahead were abandoned migrant shacks.

Cash found a way to tuck her body into the truck's bed against the wheel well so she wasn't getting thrown around quite as much. The advantage she had, she hoped—now that she could think some without getting tossed and thrown—is that she knew this part of the river. She and Wheaton fished here occasionally and even though she didn't trap gophers anymore, she used to, right along this stretch too. And when she wanted to get away from Fargo—the city lights, the drinking and pool sharking, Jim—when she wanted to get away from it all, she would come down here and walk the riverbank or just sit and listen to the mosquitoes hum, the bullfrogs talk to their lady frog friends and watch the fireflies fly.

The driver made a left turn, hit a bump. Cash lost

her tuck-in spot as her body was lifted and smacked down like a belly flop, but on metal, not water. And then the truck stopped. Cash initially felt panic, fear that this is how her life would end, shot in the head and left to rot in a burlap bag meant for potatoes. Fear that she would never have children like Josie Day Dodge had, that she would never get to ask Wheaton about her mom. Or her dad for that matter. Questions she had avoided her whole life. Cash felt cold sweat pool in the middle of her lower back and the muscles of her arms start to shake with fright. Then she was dragged by her feet to the end of the pickup truck, hauled out and tossed again over a man's shoulder.

She was tempted to pee her pants just to make him mad, but he hadn't shot her yet and fool that she was, she didn't want them to speed up the process. "Open that door for me," the guy carrying her said to his partner. Cash knew then they were going into one of the abandoned migrant shacks.

The next thing she knew she was dumped on the wire bedspring of a bed. The creaking of the springs scared her. She had a momentary flashback of her mom or someone having sex with someone. *Don't think that thought*, she thought. She was and always had been a firm believer in one of the sayings of the elders, "Be careful what you think. Your thoughts are powerful. They can create reality." And so she shut off the flashback and counted the bullets left in the box under the front seat of her truck sitting back outside Mickey's.

She was at thirteen, individually visualizing the .22 caliber marker on each brass bullet when a large hand pushed her shoulder. The man who spoke was the man who had sat in the passenger seat the night they had mistaken her for a bear.

"You think you're slick, huh, girl? Think you're living back in the Old West? A scout maybe? Thinking you can track the outlaws like Tonto? Geronimo?" He shoved her shoulder again. "Had me fooled." The man, who had been drunk that night and first mistook her for a bear, laughed, almost a giggle. "Too bad we didn't shoot you that night."

"Shuttup," said his partner. "If you hadn't been so damn drunk, you would have been able to tell the difference between a damn Indian and a bear." He sat on the end of the bed, making the springs creak. Cash started counting bullets again.

"After we saw you down in the ditch there, we checked the gopher holes. I don't know how you trap a gopher with no trap. Got me thinking, though, maybe it wasn't a bear my idiot buddy here saw the other night. So we drove down to where we were parked the other night. Walked on back down to the river."

"He found that cow trail you must have been running along," said the giggler. Cash could understand why his partner was upset with him. Just the sound of his voice was annoying as hell. The guy sitting on the bed would have been better off shooting him instead of all the other people he was doing away with.

It was then she smelled the acrid smoke. He was smoking more than cigarettes. No wonder he was giggling. So really, Cash figured, she only had one idiot to deal with.

This was the second time in a week she had been nabbed and caught by surprise. First the Day Dodge kids, now these jokers. If she got out of this alive, she was going to find a judo club and take some lessons.

"Put that shit out," said the leader.

"All right, all right, Dick. Remember when that guy at the bar said, 'Open the door for me, Richard, don't shut the door on me, Dick.'" And the giggler burst out laughing. After the bedsprings creaked, the next thing Cash heard was a *thunk* and a *thud*, the sound of someone getting slugged and hitting the floor.

"Shuttup, asshole. I'll shoot your ass. Now she knows my fucking name." Cash heard the sound of a foot connecting with a body.

"Ah, man, I'm sorry, I'm sorry. Don't shoot, come on, man. I'll throw her in the river." Cash felt the bed frame bend as he used the metal bar to pull himself back up to standing. She felt him grabbing at her legs.

"We aren't going to throw her in the river here," Dick said. Cash heard the giggler hit the thin wall of the shack. Dick must have pushed him away. "Sit down over there and let me think," he said. "I was thinking we'd shoot her, but put her body in the back end of the truck under a tarp. Once we cross the border, we throw her in the river. We've already left two bodies here. She figured out who we are, that cop Wheaton that she's always hanging around with is going to be on to us soon too."

Cash kept quiet, listening to the two men talk, trying to determine what her chances were of getting out of this situation alive. She sure as hell wasn't planning on getting drowned like a feral cat in a gunnysack, a common practice among the farmers. The cats invariably overbred. The farmers tied up the litters in a gunnysack and dumped them off a bridge into the river.

"He was in the bar asking about who folks thought

killed them two. He even asked you. He's not on to us," said the giggler, calmer now that his high had been slapped out of him. "Maybe she's already dead. Hasn't moved or said a word since we dumped her on that bed there."

Cash felt a hard slap on her ass. "You alive in there?" Dick asked loudly. He slapped her again. This time she tried to kick his hand away.

He grabbed her calf. "There we go. We were just checking. See how much of this job we still have to do. Can you talk?"

"I can't breathe inside this bag," said Cash.

The dumb one giggled. "You won't have to worry about that too much longer." Cash heard him get whacked again.

They took the bag off her. Her eyes had to adjust to the dim light of an old kerosene lamp the guys had sitting in the middle of the floor. Cash took her time looking at the two men.

Dick was close to five-eleven, about two hundred pounds, thick shoulders from doing farm labor. He was wearing jeans and a flannel work shirt, the dirty neckline of what used to be a white undershirt covered his neck front where his shirt was unbuttoned. Instead of the Red Wing work boots that most guys wore, he had on scuffed black lace-up leather boots. Dirty blond hair, a bit longer than most of the farmers around the Red River Valley. She was surprised to see a gold wedding band on his left ring finger.

The giggler, whose name she still hadn't heard, was much shorter and thinner. Five foot five at the most and weighing in as a welterweight, not more than one hundred forty-five anyways. He had on a thin cotton long-sleeved shirt with the sleeves rolled up to his elbows. He too was wearing scuffed black leather boots with his laces wrapped a couple times around the top of the boots. No wedding ring. In the dim light thrown by the kerosene lamp, she couldn't tell if his hair was dark brown or black. He had a weasel-looking face, which had made him look scary in daylight but the dope he had been smoking just made him look like—a dope.

Cash's cheek hurt where it was pressed into the wire springs. She scooted her legs over to the edge of the bed and pushed herself up to a seated position. Dick put a firm hand on her shoulder. "Where do you think you're going?" he growled.

"Nowhere."

"What were you doing the other night spying on us?"

"What are you talking about?"

"Don't play dumb. We know it was you running through the woods the other night."

"Sure, that was me, but I was just camped out down here. When your friend shouted he'd seen a bear, I got scared and took off running. You all were gonna shoot me without even knowing what or who I was."

"Come on, John saw you in the bar, then you were out here. Now today you were nosing around in the ditch. You'd be as dead as John already, but we need to know how much that county sheriff knows."

"What do you mean, knows? I don't know what he knows."

Dick pushed her back on the bed. "Don't bullshit. Everyone in town says you're his little pet."

Cash was trying desperately to think her way out of this. She lay still, gathering her thoughts. Her fingers fiddled with the rope ends that had her wrists tied behind her back. It was actually looser than what she had thought. It was worth a try to hook the knot on one of the bedsprings and attempt to loosen it. They hadn't killed her right away and now Cash was confident she was going to live. It was just a question of what it was going to take to get out of here alive.

She had one foster mother who would preach,

Where there's a will, there's a way. Those words gave her encouragement right then. As she worked the knot on the springs she assessed her situation.

She had no doubt she could take the welterweight in a fight. For one, he was stoned, slow-moving. It was the big guy she had to worry about. But these were not smart men. Neither of them had a weapon, though Dick kept threatening to shoot her or his partner. Which meant they probably had a rifle out in the cab of the truck. The door to the shack was on cheap hinges and only closed with a wire spring, which meant there wasn't a door handle she had to worry about turning. If she ever got free, she could just hit the door running.

The stoned, weasel-face guy had been sitting on the floor since the last time Dick had whacked him. He pushed himself up and started to walk toward the door, the lamplight casting a long wobbly shadow as he walked.

"Where the hell you going?"

"Gotta see a man about a horse."

"Christ."

"What? A man can't take a piss when he needs to?"

"Shuttup."

Weasel Face let the door slam behind him. Cash and

Dick heard a muffled giggle. "Don't slam the door on me Dick," he said, followed by the sound of liquid hitting the ground on the west side of the shack.

Right at that moment, they heard tires on gravel down at the road crossing. Headlights beamed in their direction. Dick put his meaty paw over Cash's mouth. Weasel Face stopped pissing mid-stream. "Dick, Dick!" he whispered loudly, "someone's coming."

"Keep your ass out there," Dick whispered back. "They can't see you on that side of the shack. And keep your damn mouth shut." He kept his hand over Cash's mouth.

Cash kept working the knot on the bedsprings. The headlights coming toward them turned off. The engine stopped. Country music drifted across the night air. Cash heard a girl's laugh. Must be a couple coming here to make out.

She could hear the weasel creeping around the outside of the shack. He must be trying to get a look at who had driven up.

"Psst, Dick. Psst."

"What, you idiot?" Dick's whisper was a growl.

"It's a couple parking. They're making out like crazy."

"Shuttup and stay out of sight."

Cash felt the knot loosen. She shifted her hips as if she were trying to get more comfortable on the springs, at the same time slipping her right hand loose from the rope. When she moved, Dick clamped harder on her mouth.

"Dick!"

"I said shuttup!"

"I gotta tell you something."

"For Christ's sake, what?"

"I can see light through the cracks of the shack."

"What?!"

"I can see light through the cracks of the shack. They know we're down here. If they come down here to see who we are, they're going to be able to see our faces. Maybe you should put that lamp out."

Goddamnit to hell, thought Cash. *Why the hell did he have to make an intelligent observation at this point?*

"I'll put it out," whispered Dick. "If you make a sound, I'll kill you with my bare hands," he threatened Cash. She shook her head in agreement, signaling she would stay quiet. He took his hand away and then started to stand up to reach the lamp to put it out. Cash grabbed his belt and pulled him back onto the bed as hard as she could. *Shit, he was heavy.* He hit the bed with a *thud*, the old metal frame crashing to the floor, with Cash underneath him. *Oh good lord, he was heavy.*

"Get the fucking gun!" Dick yelled. Rolling off Cash as fast as his weight would allow, but still on the floor with Cash where the bed had crashed down, he went to grab her upper arms but in the rush only grabbed her jacket sleeves. Cash played dead. She flopped limply as he jerked her toward him, he with his knees on either side of her on the floor trying to gain control. Cash heard the pickup door slam right outside the shack. In that same instant, the headlights of the vehicle down the road were turned on.

"Bitch!" screamed Dick as he attempted to slap her alongside the head. Cash, who was close enough to feel his arm muscles tighten had anticipated it and flopped her head so his palm grazed the top of her head. Short as she was, lying between his larger frame, she realized her knees were in the proximity of his crotch. From that dead limp state, feet still tied together, using all the adrenaline pumping through her body, she kneed Dick in the groin as hard as she could. Dick collapsed on her. He screamed, a deep guttural sound, as he rolled off her, his hands grabbing his crotch. She ripped her jean jacket off and wrapped and tied it over his face, pulling the sleeves and knotting them as fast and as tight as she could.

"They're coming, Dick! What should I do?" hollered the weasel.

Cash fumbled with the knot at her ankles as Dick rolled in agony. She elbowed him in the head as hard as she could to buy herself some more time. She got one foot free, grabbed the lit kerosene lamp and threw it on Dick.

Like she had planned, she hit the door running and kept right on. Behind her she heard indiscernible yells and screams. She looked back as she hit the tree line. She saw Dick run out of the shack, flames lapping up his left side. He dropped and rolled across the field. The shack was going up in flames and Weasel Face was shooting at the car that had come down the road. The car made a U-turn down into the shallow ditch and sped off. Cash heard the gravel spit even as she ran, lungs burning, stumbling across dead branches and tree roots until she felt the cow path underfoot.

Her braid whipped against her back. She reached and grabbed it over her shoulder, tucked it into her jeans in front. She didn't want to get slowed down by it hooking on a tree branch. In the distance, she could hear Dick swearing and moaning. When she got to the fallen tree, she clambered over it just like she had the other night, but this time, rather than stopping to pee, she kept on running. She knew at the next bend of the river was the backside of the old county dump. That would put her by the gravel road about three and a half miles north of town. There were no trees along the road until you got to a couple farmsteads.

SHE SLOWED TO A FAST walk, breathing hard, hand on her right side where she was getting a stitch. She heard Dick's pickup truck start and the roll of its wheels over the dirt and grass road. She stopped to focus, listening. If she could trust her ears, the truck was moving away from her. Dick must be burned pretty bad if they were hightailing it to the county hospital in Ada and not stopping to look for her. She ran up the riverbank, pulling herself forward on saplings and river brush. By the time she got to the tree line, all she could see were the pickup taillights heading due east.

Fools. Desperate fools. She ran across the wheat field where they had dumped Tony O and—at a steady pace—ran south toward Halstad. Flames from the shack were lighting up the night sky. Halfway to town, she met the volunteer fire department truck on its way to put out the fire. They slowed when they saw her but she shouted, "Go put it out! I'm okay!" and kept running. *Damn cigarettes*, she thought, her lungs burning. When she hit the pavement of the first street, she ran past the church, onto Main Street, then down to Mickey's.

"Gimme the phone, gimme the phone," she shouted at the bartender, the front door of the bar slamming behind her.

He took one look at her, pulled the black rotary phone from behind the counter and set it up on the bar between two drinkers. Cash grabbed it and dialed the county jail. No damn answer. Next she called Wheaton's house. He answered on the fifth ring.

Without preamble, Cash said, "They're going to the county hospital. One of them's burnt bad. I'm on my way there." And she hung up, shoved the phone back across the bar and took a big swig of the guy's beer to her right. She pushed back from the bar and ran to the side door.

Behind her she heard, "She must have been at the fire."

"She looks like she's been in a fight."

"You okay, Cash?" someone hollered after her.

She waved a hand in the air, pushed out through the screen door, digging her keys out of her pocket as she ran.

The first thing she did when she opened the truck door was grab her .22, take the safety off and make sure it was loaded. She put the rifle on the seat beside her, barrel pointed toward the bottom passenger side. She spun on gravel backing out of the parking spot, bouncing over the railroad tracks before she shifted gears and grabbed the sliding rifle all at the same time as she took off for Ada.

The Ranchero was in high gear and the gas pedal pushed to the floor. She whipped past one car and flashed her high beams at another one that threatened to pull out on to the main road from a side country road. Halfway to Ada, she calmed enough to punch in the cigarette lighter and then realized that her cigarettes were still in the jean jacket she had wrapped around Dick's head. *Shit!* She leaned over and rummaged through the glove box searching for an extra pack. No dice. Without letting up on the gas, she reached under the truck seat. Sometimes she threw a pack under there. Nothing. She dug through the ashtray to find the longest butt she could, straightened it out to all of one inch and lit up.

Ada was up ahead. She could see the lights. *How many times had she been in this town today?* She'd lost track. She didn't slow until she hit the outskirts of town. Then she only slowed to sixty and headed straight to the county hospital.

She pulled in next to Wheaton's cruiser and jumped out of the truck, grabbed the rifle and headed around the hospital to the back door. She walked down the linoleum hallway, listening for voices, feeling the adrenaline, sensing the air for Wheaton. She saw a couple nurses going in and out of doors at the end of the hallway and headed that way. As she got closer she smelled burnt hair and heard moaning, another male voice and Wheaton's deeper one. She could also hear Doc Felix saying, "Toasted marshmallow. You look like a toasted marshmallow, son."

Cash shook her head back and forth. She was going to have to remember to not shoot the doc. She reminded herself of that as she reached the doorway and looked in.

WHEATON TURNED HIS HEAD AROUND to see her. He wasn't in uniform, but he had his gun belt on and handcuffs stuffed in his pockets. The smaller guy, the one whose name she never got, was standing on the opposite side of the bed, Wheaton blocking his view of the doorway.

Wheaton asked, "How'd this happen, boy? You fall in a bonfire?"

Moaning followed.

Doc said, "I've shot him full of morphine, so I don't think he's going to answer any questions, Wheaton."

"Who you need to question is that damn Indian bitch who lit him on fire," said the other guy.

"And why would that be?" asked Wheaton.

"We were going north of town a bit to have a few beers, enjoy the stars and she followed us out there."

"How'd this fire happen?" Wheaton asked.

"I don't know. She had a Coleman lantern or maybe one of those old kerosene lanterns. We were in one of those migrant shacks."

"Kinda hard to see the stars from in there," commented Wheaton.

"We had just gone in to look around, curious, you know. Then she came up on us. Started accusing us of killing that Indian a week ago. And of killing that kid you all found dumped in the ditch out that way. She was screaming and threatening us. Dick here walked towards her to try and quiet her down and that's when she threw the kerosene lamp on him and took off running. All I could do was roll him on the ground to put out the flames and throw him in the truck and get over this way to the doc."

Doc Felix started to stand up from leaning over Dick. Cash stepped back and over so that she was hidden from his view. Doc Felix said, "I'm going to have to call one of the ambulance drivers in to take him to St. Luke's in Fargo. He might have some fourth-degree burns and they have better equipment."

"How long you think it's going to take?" asked Wheaton.

"About a half hour to get 'em up and rolling," answered Doc Felix.

"And what's your name, son?" Wheaton asked the weasel-faced guy.

"Clyde, Clyde Svenson."

"What else can you tell me about all this, Clyde?" asked Wheaton.

"Nothing. You should be out looking for that wild Indian. Last I saw she was hightailing down the riverbank. The other night she was spying on us too. Made us think she was a bear until we went back down there earlier today and saw her footprints. Damn lucky she didn't get shot. Then she was down in the ditch where that young kid was found. Tried to tell us she was trapping gophers."

Cash leaned against the wall. *What is Wheaton doing letting this guy talk on and on?* But right then, the two feds, dressed in identical suits to the ones they were wearing every other time she had seen them, came walking around a corner down by the main hospital door. Cash moved the rifle as best she could back behind her leg that was farthest from them. Their leather shoes clacked on the linoleum floor.

Wheaton must have heard them too because he poked his head out around the doorway and waved them on down. At the same time, he said behind him, "You just wait there, son."

Wheaton pointed at a leather-covered chair at the closest end of the hallway, indicating that Cash was to go there. As the two men passed Cash, they hesitated and looked at her suspiciously. Wheaton said, "She's with me," and motioned for them to go into the hospital room. Cash waited until the two men walked past, and then she moved and plopped down in the chair. She put the safety on the rifle and laid it on the floor under the chair, back against the wall. She put her elbows on her knees and her head on her hands and drifted into a meditative state. The dreams, the sensations, going to Josie's house, getting tripped up by the Day Dodge kids, the sorrow in their eyes, walking in the ditch, running along the hardened clay of the cow path with her braid whapping her on the back, Long Braids and pool shots—all this flitted through Cash's consciousness until she saw the tips of scuffed work boots standing in front of her.

She looked up into Wheaton's face, an evening stubble evident on his chin. She leaned around him and saw the weasel in handcuffs being led down the hall by one of the feds. The other fed was walking alongside a metal gurney an attendant was wheeling down the hall.

Dick's body was draped under white sheets, his face sooty and his hair sticking up in weird directions. An IV ran down a metal pole attached to the gurney.

Wheaton pulled Cash to her feet, then reached behind the chair for her rifle and handed it to her. He put his arm around her shoulder and said, "I have to take you over to the station and get a statement from you."

As they passed the hospital room Dick and Clyde had been in, Doc Felix was standing in the doorway, leaning against the doorjamb. He shook his head like he didn't believe what he was seeing. Cash glared at him until he turned back into the room. Wheaton walked her out to his cruiser.

"Can we stop at the liquor store so I can get a pack of cigarettes?" she asked.

Wheaton drove to the liquor store, got out, went in and came back with a pack of Marlboros. He handed the pack to Cash. She whacked the filter end of the pack against the thumb edge of her left hand to tamp the tobacco tighter into the cigarettes. Then she zipped the gold plastic thread around the cellophane and folded open one end. She tapped the pack again got out a cigarette and lit up.

By that time they were back at the jail, Cash got out. Wheaton opened the back door and carried in her rifle. She walked into the open cell, grabbed one of the wool blankets off the bed, folded it and put it on one end of the wooden bench she had come to think of as hers. She pulled the tall round visitor ashtray over by the bench and lay down.

Wheaton was making a pot of coffee in the back room. When he came out, he opened a desk drawer and got a sheaf of papers and a flat box of carbon paper. He stacked paper, carbon, paper about five, six times, then put one set into the typewriter. He went and brought out two cups of steaming coffee. He set one in the round ashtray for Cash and put the other on the desk as he sat down in front of the typewriter. He looked at Cash.

Lying on her back, she blew a stream of cigarette smoke up toward the ceiling.

Wheaton said, "Why don't we start with the rope that's still tied around your left wrist."

Cash lifted her arm and, *goddamn*, there was the twine they had used to tie her up, still wrapped around her wrist. So that's where she started. She talked through the night's story while Wheaton clacked away at the Underwood Five typewriter.

Three cups of coffee and seven cigarettes later, Wheaton unrolled the last page out of the typewriter. He asked her to sign and date the last page. He sorted the originals from the carbons, carefully putting the carbons back in the thin flat box he had taken them out of. Saving taxpayer dollars, Cash guessed. Then he stapled both the originals and the carbon copy. He put the latter in a locked file behind the desk and the original in a manila envelope.

"I'll give this to the feds tomorrow," he said standing up. "I'm going to lock it in my cruiser so it doesn't get misplaced between now and then. Come on. You okay to drive home, or you going to sleep on your bed there?"

Cash swung her feet off the bench and sat back up. "I'm good," she answered. "I want to sleep in my own bed. And I think tomorrow—or maybe now it's today—I have to go register for classes."

"It's not that late. Not even closing time. Which doesn't mean you still have time to go to the bar." Wheaton reached behind himself and pulled out Cash's rifle. He checked the safety and then handed it to her. "Glad you're alive, kid."

"Me too." She walked out of the jail to her Ranchero, climbed in, turned on the ignition, shifted into gear and drove into Fargo. At her apartment, she put the rifle under her bed, dropped all her clothes as was her fashion and soaked for about ten minutes in a steaming hot bathtub. She climbed out, washed her hair in the kitchen sink and crawled into bed. Just as she was dozing off, she remembered to reach out and set the alarm for 7:00 A.M. She didn't want to be late to register.

WHEN THE ALARM WENT OFF in the morning after too few hours of sleep, she had a hard time adjusting to the sunlight streaming in through the windows. She swung her feet out of bed and felt the soreness in her thighs and calves from the run into town the night before. She got dressed and thought *damn*, she would have to go by JCPenney's and get a new jean jacket sometime today. She opened her top drawer and pulled out her money sock, got out a twenty and stuffed it into her jeans pocket, her driver's license in her back pocket, and she was off.

At the college there were long lines of young white kids walking to the administration building. Some were dressed as if they were ready to go to church. Others sported long hair, hip-hugger bell-bottoms, and paisley shirts or blouses. There were jocks and cheerleader types. Cash's chest tightened.

The room was crowded. You were supposed to stand in the line behind the first letter of your last name. Signs were taped up—A–E, F–J and on through the alphabet. She was surprised to see kids standing in the line for Zs. She had never met anyone whose last name started with a Z. Cash felt the adrenaline building in her body. She started to walk out, then thought of Wheaton driving over to the education building on the reservation, getting the paperwork and filling it out. All she had to do was stand in line and she would be in. She went back and stood behind the A–E sign.

The lines inched forward. Some of the kids sat on the floor, backpacks embroidered with peace signs. They scooted forward as the line moved, hefting their backpacks with them. Cash had picked up the papers with all the possible classes from a table as you entered the building. As she waited, she looked over the catalog trying to figure out which classes she was going to take. While some kids had their forms all filled out, some were poring over the papers as hard as she was.

A short blond, blue-eyed girl was standing behind her. She was wearing the widest bell-bottoms Cash had ever seen with flowers embroidered up and down the legs. She was also wearing a beaded headband. She caught Cash looking at her and said, "Do you know what you're taking?"

Cash said, "No."

"Are you a freshman?"

"Yes."

Then the hippie girl proceeded to tell Cash how she could read the sheet to know which classes were for freshman, which were required classes for freshman and that it probably didn't matter anyway, 'cause Cash would need to find an advisor, and if the classes were full, she would need to add and drop classes, which everyone did anyways the first two weeks, and how her boyfriend was a sophomore and he had told her which teachers were the easy teachers and how you wanted to set up your school schedule so you didn't have any classes on Monday mornings or Friday afternoons, that way you always had a long weekend for partying, and did she smoke pot?

When Cash shook her head no, the girl said, "Not yet, and my name is Sharon Bakkus. What's your name?"

"Cash."

"Cash? Like in money, Cash?"

"I guess."

Before the girl could ask another question, the line had moved forward enough for Cash to hand in her paperwork. She got a handful of stamped papers back and was told that she would have to go meet with the Indian advisor, Mrs. Kills Horses, in Room 106 to make sure that her scholarship money came in and would pay for her classes.

Sharon, who had moved herself forward to stand by Cash as if they were best buddies said, "I know where that is. My boyfriend is from Turtle Mountain and we hung out there all last year. Wait and I'll walk over with you."

Cash didn't know what else to do so she waited while Sharon registered for her classes.

When they got to Room 106, Sharon introduced her to Mrs. Kills Horses, a tall Lakota woman wearing a dress with a belt that had silver conches on it. She wore nylons, heels and the longest beaded earrings Cash had ever seen. While Mrs. Kills Horses seemed nice enough and explained how her money would come and be disbursed through the financial aid office, Sharon piped in and let her know she knew where that was.

Mrs. Kills Horses continued. Cash had to carry a twelve-course load and make at least a C average to keep her financial aid. While they were chattering at her, Cash again felt the tightening in her chest and a headache, the worst kind of hangover headache, creep up the back of her head.

She interrupted and asked, "Am I done for today?"

"Well," said Sharon, "you could go to the bookstore and get your books. Although if you wait a couple days until you get the syllabus from your teachers, you'll know exactly which books to get—sometimes they change the syllabus at the last minute and if you wait you won't have to return—"

"I gotta go," interrupted Cash and walked out of Mrs. Kills Horses's office. She looked down the hall for an exit sign, saw one and headed for it. She pushed open the door and gulped fresh air. She bounced down two concrete stairs and stepped out on to the green grass of the campus mall, surrounded on either side by thick stately oaks. She could tell each one had been strategically planted along the winding sidewalks between the red brick buildings. Even with groups of students sitting on the grass, leaning against their trunks, the trees seemed lonely. Nothing like the oaks along the river that grew where they wanted to grow and leaned in and touched each other with their middle branches, whose voices sang through their leaves like the hum of electric wires running alongside the country roads.

These campus trees were like Mrs. Kills Horses, dressed up in church clothes, their leaves saying, I am an oak, the same way Mrs. Kills Horses earrings and belt said, I am an Indian, but everything else said something else.

Cash walked quickly to her Ranchero. Lit up as soon as she got to the truck and stood there leaning against the cab, looking back toward the college and down at the papers in her hand. English 101. Psych 101. Science 101. And Judo. That would fulfill her physical education requirement.

She inhaled and blew smoke. *Could she do this?* Wheaton thought she could. She flicked the cigarette into the street, got into her truck and drove to Shari's Kitchen for some breakfast.

After that she drove to the JCPenney in the new mall on the west side of Fargo and bought herself a jean jacket. She would have to wash it a hundred times to get it as soft as the one that she had wrapped around Dick's head.

She had noticed that most of the girls at the college were wearing platform shoes. Big clunky shoes with two-inch wedges. On the way out of the store, she saw a pair that kind of looked like work boots but were women's shoes with platform heels. She stopped and asked the salesclerk if she could try them on. Cash grew two inches in three minutes. She strutted in front of the mirror, took the shoes off, put them back in the box, folding the white tissue paper over them.

"Should I ring those up for you?" asked the clerk.

"No, I was just looking."

"Those are the shoes everyone is buying."

"Yeah, I've seen that," said Cash, "but I just brought enough money to get a new jacket."

Cash had also noticed that the girls at the college dressed like girls. She had felt out of place standing in line in her straight leg blue jeans, T-shirt, hooded sweatshirt and tennis shoes. She realized she looked more like a farm boy than a college girl. Even the hippie chick Sharon looked more like a girl than she did.

Cash walked out of JCPenney's and into the mall proper. She looked in store windows. She never shopped. Everything she did in life was out of necessity. If it wasn't necessary, she didn't do it. She had never even thought about different clothes, different shoes. Now she looked.

At the other end of the mall was a restaurant, with a low brick wall. You could look over it and see the customers dining. As Cash walked past, she saw a familiar head bent toward a little girl in a high chair. When she looked back, she had to think twice about who it was. Seeing Jim here, in a family restaurant, was so out of context that she had to adjust her thinking to the image she was seeing now. Not Jim bent over a pool table or Jim sitting on the edge of her bed slipping off his clothes, but Jim sitting in a restaurant surrounded by three little girls.

Blond hair brushed and held back behind their ears with little plastic barrettes. The woman with him was as blond as the girls, smiling at Jim as he put a spoonful of food in his baby's mouth. Cash turned quickly before he would look up, spun around and headed toward the mall's main exit.

She didn't know what to think about it, so she didn't. She just got in her Ranchero and drove back to her apartment. As she got out of her truck, there was Wheaton in a brown Chevy station wagon. He smiled and said, "Hey, those federal guys called me this morning and asked me to bring your statement into town here for them. I dropped it off about a half hour ago. Thought I might catch you and see if you wanted to go have breakfast."

"I already ate."

"Well, maybe we could walk on over to the Silver Cup. I could buy you a cup of coffee and I could grab a bite to eat. Catch you up on the latest about those two jokers."

"All right." She fell into step beside him on the sidewalk. They didn't say anything until they were seated in the hole-in-the-wall diner and the waitress had set down glasses of water and a cup of coffee for Wheaton. Wheaton pulled out the menu that was slid between the sugar container and the salt and pepper shakers. Cash could see he didn't really read it.

"I think I'll just get the hot roast beef sandwich.

You sure you don't want anything? I'm buying." He looked at her. He was tall and fit just right in his side of the booth. Cash felt like a child with her feet only touching the floor if she stretched the tips of her feet downward.

"I just ate. Maybe a piece of blueberry pie. Yeah, I'll have a piece of pie."

"Did you get registered for classes?"

"Yeah." She stared at the water glass.

"What?"

"I just don't know."

"Don't know what?"

"I just don't know. Christ, I sound like a whiner."

Wheaton raised an eyebrow in question. "A whiner?"

"You know, those kids at the Drive-Inn who always want a malt and an ice-cream cone with their hamburger and pout when their moms don't let them."

The waitress came over and stood at the booth, pencil and pad in hand. Wheaton placed their order, adding more coffee for himself and a Coke for Cash. When she walked away, he asked, "So what don't you know?"

"If I can go to school. They're all so . . . I don't know, white."

"So are the men in the fields."

"Yeah, but they're just men. This is like going back to high school. Cheerleaders and churchgoers. And hippies, lots of hippies in bell-bottoms."

"Cash, we've had this conversation before. You're too smart to let them get to you. All you got to do is get your butt to class, one day at a time, get a degree and you can do something besides drive a damn grain truck the rest of your life."

And then he played his trump card. The card he never played. "I didn't carry you out of that ditch for nothing, keep a little girl in jail overnight. I pretend I don't know about the fake ID that gets you into the bars. I'm a sheriff, for chrissake. I signed the papers as your guardian so you can live off campus. I didn't do any of that 'cause I have to, Cash. You're too smart, too good to waste yourself in the fields."

Cash didn't want to cry so she grinned at him and said, "I could just shoot pool for a living."

Wheaton looked at her over his coffee cup.

"I'm just kidding," she said. "I'll go. I'll go. Some hippie chick with an Indian boyfriend showed me how to fill out the paperwork and where the Indian students' office is. So I just got to show up after the long weekend and start classes."

"What are you taking?"

"A lot of 101s. Apparently there are required courses you have to take before you can take the classes you really want to take. I did sign up for judo as my physical education class though. I need that after the two times this past week I got my butt kicked."

"Well, looks like you kicked butt anyways. Glad you're okay."

"So what's happening with those two?"

Wheaton finished chewing the food in his mouth, then he set his fork down. "Well, Clyde kept talking once the feds got him. It's such a stupid story. I just don't understand how men could behave so badly. Anyways, they're both from Canada, Clyde and Richard. They came down here and were working the fields out at Arnie's. Staying in the bunkhouse. Apparently a couple of the other Indian guys had been drinking with these two bozos on the weekends, and these two would weasel them out of most of their paychecks once they got too drunk. Guess they planned to do the same thing with Tony O. He had been living on money he had brought on down with him, saving his two-week checks to cash all at one time before he went back up north for the winter."

Wheaton took another bite of his hot roast beef,

chewing and looking out the window of the Silver Cup. "They tried to get him to go out drinking with him. He wouldn't. Said for once in their lives his kids were going to have decent clothes to go to school in. He was going to even stop at some florist shop in Bemidji and get his wife a bouquet of real roses. Apparently, Dick lost his head, couldn't stand the thought of an Indian standing up to him, saying no, so he just lost it from what Clyde says, and when Tony O went to walk away from them, Dick stabbed him. This was over in a dirt field just outside of town here. They didn't want to leave the body there, lord knows why, so they took it and dumped it in the field where he was found."

"And what about the other guy?" asked Cash.

"Dick was afraid he was going to talk. He was from some small town over there in North Dakota—Rugby maybe. Small town way up there close to the Canadian border. Guess they killed him just to shut him up. They were going to pick up their last work check and head over the boundary. We would have never caught them then. Just what the heck were you doing out spying on them in the middle of the night anyways?"

"I just had a hunch, Wheaton. Was just trying to help you out. You said you wanted to figure it out before the feds did. And you did." Cash filled her mouth with more blueberry pie.

"Well, it's done," Wheaton said. "And Dick is going to live. He'll be over here at St. Luke's, or they might drive him down to the Cities until his burns have healed, then they'll both go to trial. The feds will keep the case. With them being Canucks and all, it's an international situation."

"Hmmm."

Wheaton went back to eating his sandwich. Cash finished her pie. As she pushed the plate away, she said, "Did you know that the school has a major in criminal justice?"

From the way Wheaton said no, Cash didn't know if she quite believed him.

When Wheaton finished eating, he put some dollar bills under his plate. They got up, left the café and walked back to her apartment.

Wheaton stood by his car with the door opened. Cash stood on the sidewalk.

"I called the phone company. Someone should be by later today to install the wiring," he said.

When Cash tilted her head in question, he said, "Well, I figured you'll need to be putting more time into studying, not running back and forth between

Ada and here. This way, if you need something, you can just call. I put the phone in my name. That way if the school checks, they'll see that both the phone and the rent are in my name. Proof that you're not living some wild single life." He laughed and got into the car, then leaned back out. "And A's. I expect A's."

With that, he backed out and drove off.

Cash went upstairs. Cleaned her rifle. Cleaned her bathroom. Cleaned her bedroom/living room. Cleaned her kitchen. When the phone company showed up late in the afternoon, the floors were swept and mopped and the bathroom gleamed. Cash asked for a pale beige phone installed with a cord long enough so the phone could sit on the dresser in the bedroom, but she could walk into the kitchen with it.

After the phone guy left, she sat on the edge of her bed next to the phone. Without lifting the receiver, she put her index finger in the little round holes over the numbers and starting at one, spun each number around. It made a small clicking sound. Then she picked up the phone book the guy had left. She looked up the number for the appliance store she lived above. *Huh*, she thought, she could call the landlord and tell him to turn up the heat this winter, instead of going downstairs and asking him face to face.

The only two numbers she knew, in the whole wide world, were the Norman County Jail and Wheaton's home number. She lifted the receiver and listened to the dial tone. She dialed a one and listened to the sound the number made inside the receiver. She hung up and set the whole thing back on the dresser next to her alarm clock.

Tonight was also the pool tournament over at the Flame. Cash got up off the bed. An hour later she was bathed, dressed in jeans tucked inside the cowboy boots with a clean shirt on under the new jean jacket. She brushed and braided her hair in two long braids down her back, which she then hooked together with a rubber band at the end of the tails.

Then, instead of driving, she walked on over to the Casbah. She kicked the screen door back behind her to make sure her hair didn't get caught. Keep those old men pushing the same quarter back and forth between them. No sense letting one of them win all the time.

Ol' man Willie had a head start on her by a long shot. Shorty put two Buds on the bar so all she had to do was put her money in his hand, take the bottles and head on over to the tables. No other players were there yet, which was just how Cash wanted it. She wanted to get in a few practice games before heading over to the tournament at the Flame.

She dropped her quarters in the slot, kept kneeling while the balls dropped and she put them up in the table in the rack. She practiced her bank shots the first game against herself. The second game she focused just on her English, hitting the cue ball a little left or right of center, trying to control the spin of the ball it hit. By then another player had come into the bar and put up his quarters. When she was done playing herself, she chalked up while he racked and then broke the rack with a solid *thwack*. She won solidly but drained her second beer and conceded the table to him. She broke down her cue, put it back in its case and waved to Shorty that she was out of there.

She walked the six blocks to the Flame just for the hell of it. The lights were low, all except up on the stripper stage, where some blonde wearing silver sparkly remnants gyrated to an Elvis tune. Whereas most bars had one—at the most two—pool tables, the Flame had eight tables which allowed them to host larger pool tournaments. Cash found the registration table and signed in, noting that Jim had already signed them up and paid the ten-dollar registration fee. All the money went into a pot that was allocated for first, second and third place. If they won tonight, she would walk out with next month's rent. She looked around and saw him bent over a table along the farthest wall.

She stood and looked at him bank the 9 and cut the 2-ball into the side pocket. This is how she was used to seeing him— until this week she hadn't thought of him outside of the context of smoke, beers, hardwood floors and green velvet with blue chalk stains on his index fingers. *Hm.* She hoped the image of him leaning over and feeding his daughter wasn't imprinted in her mind forever. She walked over to join him. She took her cue out of its case and chalked up.

"There you are, Cash. I was starting to get a little worried you wouldn't show up."

"I gotta make next month's rent," Cash said, rolling her cue on the table behind her, making sure it hadn't warped.

For the next three hours, they shot pool and drank beers. Quite a number of the guys lost early, too distracted by the dancers on stage to stay in the zone required to keep winning. There were a couple other women players, regulars at the tournaments. Cash was on a nodding and *good shot* basis with them. They wore their jeans tight and their hair ratted and sprayed up in Dolly Parton curls. But a couple of them were damn good pool players. Kept Cash on her game.

Cash was focused. Jim was distracted. He missed a couple easy runs and they lost and had to play in the elimination bracket. Less win money but still the rent if they came in first. At least she was drinking free. Her stomach knotted, apprehension did cartwheels in her stomach. The headache that had threatened to rise full force at the college was back at the base of her neck. Cash was getting mad at how sloppy Jim was playing.

"Come on, Jim," she said, "get in the game. This is my rent I'm playing for here. I don't have daddy's farmhouse to go home to." The beer in her talked.

She could tell by the way his face reddened she had hurt his feelings. "Aw, man, come on, Jim. I was just kidding. Come on, let's just win this one."

When he finished a short run, but short of the 8, he walked back to the wall and took a long swig of his beer. Cash walked over to him and put her arm around his waist. "Come on, I'm sorry. I just want to win. You know how I get."

Jim put his arm around her shoulders and pulled her close, kissed the top of her head. "Just got a few things on my mind, Cash. Grab that waitress to bring us a couple more beers."

Cash took his money and held it up for the waitress to see. She nodded and headed back to the bar. A new stripper, this one wearing red lingerie, was just walking on stage. The men lining the stage were catcalling and whistling. One of the women pool players mocked the stripper's walk, getting the guys she was playing against hooting and hollering. She then proceeded to run the table on them.

Cash laughed and handed the waitress the money in exchange for two more Buds.

Cash handed Jim his beer. They stood drinking, smoking and waiting until their game was called. Jim wasn't playing any better. They were coming up on closing time and last game and last call and he had to either make it or break it, and he goddamn broke it by sinking the cue right behind the 8-ball on the last game that would have had them place in the tournament. Cash had ordered her usual two at closing time.

She had tucked one in the waist of her jeans at the small of her back, intending to drink it on the way home. As she broke down her cue, Jim kept apologizing and trying to put his arm around her and kiss her neck and she just kept getting angrier. *Goddamn loser*, she was thinking as she swatted away his arm.

When he said, "Come on, let's go," Cash answered, "Nah, I'll get myself home tonight."

While Jim just stood there, the waitress walked up to Cash and said, "You need to leave those beers here."

"What?"

"That beer you stashed in your purse. You need to leave the beer here. No one can leave the bar with an open bottle."

"I don't have a goddamn purse. Never carry a goddamn purse," said Cash, all the while aware of the cold bottle pressed against her lower back.

"No trouble, just get the bottle out of your purse and set it on the table," said the waitress, as a third stripper dressed as a nurse danced to Chuck Berry.

"Let it go, Cash," said Jim. "Just do what she says."

Cash felt the headache and alcohol and loss explode into her skull. "I don't have a goddamn purse!" she yelled, flinging her arms wide to show she didn't have one.

The waitress was way dumber than she looked. "Just get the bottle out of your purse and put it on the table," she said again.

All the while Jim was babbling to Cash to calm down and give the woman the bottle and just take it easy.

In one motion Cash grabbed her cue case and swept all the bottles and glasses off the table in front of her. She then proceeded to run out of the bar, clearing any tables of beer bottles and glasses within her reach with her right forearm. She heard yelling and screams of *stop!* behind her but she was still running when she hit the sidewalk and turned through the Flame parking lot. She dodged around cars, not bothering to look back to see if anyone was chasing her. And then smack, she ran straight into a much taller body than hers.

"Whoa, girl! Where you going?"

It was Long Braids. *What the hell was he doing here?* She grabbed him by the forearm and said, "Run."

He didn't stop her, just joined her in running through downtown alleys until finally they reached the railroad tracks. Cash slowed down to a sprint and kept going until she reached a trestle that ran over the Red River. Finally, she came to a walk, then walked through a trail in the brush until they reached a clearing where they could sit and look down at the river. Cash pulled the beer out from her back waistband, laughing as she felt the wetness of her jeans where the beer had spilled out and down her butt as she ran. The bottle was still three-quarters full though. She handed it to Long Braids and flopped on the ground to catch her breath, laughing.

He took a drink and said, "Why are we running?"

Cash was still laughing, couldn't stop. When she tried to take a drink, beer splashed out her nose.

"What the hell are you doing here?" she asked when she caught a breath.

"Just dropping by to see you before I head out east. Gonna see if I can join that American Indian Movement down in Minneapolis. Heard they're planning some kind of protest out on the East Coast this fall."

"Oh really? How the hell did you find me?"

"When we were in Fargo, I kept the matchbook you had. It said the Casbah. I stopped by there first and the bartender told me you were playing in a tournament over at the Flame. So I went over there."

"I see," said Cash. "Why were you standing around outside the Flame?"

Long Braids took another drink as she passed him the bottle. "I was actually inside most of the night. But you were pretty intent on winning. I didn't want to break your concentration. Besides, I wasn't too sure what was going on between you and the white guy. I thought I'd try to catch you as you were leaving, so I went outside to find your Ranchero, but didn't see it."

"He's a friend. I walked."

"What the hell happened that sent you hightailing it out of there?"

"Stupid, stupid stuff. The waitress accused me of sticking a beer bottle in my purse to carry it out of the bar." Cash started laughing. "I don't carry a purse." She finished the beer and threw the bottle in a high arc out towards the river. They heard it splash.

"Guess I'll be 86'd out of the Flame for a while. Damn shame, that's where I make my rent money."

Cash stood up and brushed the leaves and dirt off her butt and turned to walk back up the bank. Long Braids did the same. "Where we going?" he asked. Cash didn't answer, just kept walking.

He followed.

AUTHOR'S NOTE

The historical trauma Native people live with today was not a path of their own choosing. From 1819 to 1934, Native children were systematically removed from families and put into boarding schools.

There they grew up like prisoners of war, punished for speaking their languages, punished for talking to their siblings if they crossed paths. A hundred and fifteen years of children not seeing a mom and dad raise children. One hundred and fifteen years of children growing up not knowing how to hold a baby or protect a toddler. What they learned was to settle disagreements with silence, withdrawal or violence.

Then they were sent home to the newly created

reservation system where up until the mid-1960s, it was common practice for county and state social workers to scoop up Native children and remove them to white foster or adoptive homes. Sandy White Hawk, Director of the First Nations Repatriation Institute, says, "I cannot imagine the entitlement the social worker must have felt to walk into a family and just take a child. I cannot imagine how emasculating it must have been for our men to watch that happen and not be able to do anything. My uncle remembers the social worker driving into our driveway, getting out of the car and taking me."

White Hawk relates how on a national level 25–35% of Native children were taken and placed in non-Indian homes or institutions. In Minnesota, one in four were removed. White Earth and Red Lake reservations experienced higher removals. For each lost child, there is a set of grieving parents, siblings, grandparents, aunties and uncles.

As members of sovereign tribal governments, Native American children have a unique political status that was reaffirmed with the passage of the Indian Child Welfare Act of 1978. With this Act of Congress, "ICWA sets federal requirements that apply to state child custody proceedings involving an Indian child who is a member of or eligible for membership in a federally recognized tribe." Each child, by Act of Congress, should have state welfare agencies work in the best interest of the child to place the child with a family member or extended family of the tribe.

This Act was not in place during Cash's lifetime. While this is a book of fiction, the story of removal, heartbreak, post-traumatic-stress symptoms and generational trauma Cash exhibits are all too true. What is equally true of so many survivors of that time is Cash's resiliency in the face of such extreme early trauma.

You will find more information on these websites:

http://www.edweek.org/ew/projects/2013/native-american-education/history-of-american-indian-education.html

http://www.wearecominghome.com http://www.nicwa.org/Indian_Child_Welfare_Act/history

ACKNOWLEDGMENTS

So many people have made it possible for me to write. First, the "eat and meet" writing group, started by Babs with Ellen and Ida. Next the "Sunday morning writes" at Diego's abode. And the group with Diane, Nora, Mai Neng and Donna who read this manuscript over and over. Danny, who has always believed in my writing. Eileen, thanks are not enough. Jeanne and Liz: State Fair, foster kids and North Shore. And ALL the women in my life who have helped with children, food and emotional sustenance, you are in my heart forever.

Continue reading for a preview of

GIRL GONE
MISSING

Cash pulled herself up and out of her bedroom window. Her heart beat in her ears and she shivered uncontrollably. She took off running barefoot, zig-zagging across the damp ground. Her eyes darted left and right. She ran toward the plowed field, in the direction that led to town. Her foot sank into the cold, wet dirt of the furrowed field. When she tried to pull her foot up, her front leg sank into the dirt even deeper. She threw herself forward, clawing at the mud with bare hands, hearing the heavy, labored breathing of the person chasing her. Fear forced her from her body so that she was soon flying above herself. She looked back to see who was chasing her, but all she could see *was a body, the face obscured in the darkness. She looked down and could see herself stretched out in the mud below, buried to her knees, arms flailing. Some of her long brown hair was tangled up in her hands as she struggled to steady herself. But the body changed abruptly: no longer her struggling, not a short, dark-haired Indian girl, but a pale, tall and bony blonde, who looked up at Cash and screamed, "Help me!"*

ON THAT SUNNY NOTE, CASH crawled out of bed, got dressed and headed from Fargo to the Moorhead State campus on the other side of the Red River bridge. She nursed a tepid cup of coffee, intended to get her through her first two classes, while she tried to shake the dream from her head.

With a one-hour break between her biology and psychology classes, Cash made a beeline for her Ranchero and retrieved her cue stick from its usual place—behind the front seat. She took off across campus to the Student Union, heading for the billiard room.

It was beet-hauling season in the Valley, and Cash was driving beet truck afternoons and evenings when her class schedule allowed. Between classes she would stop at the rec hall to practice her game.

The rec hall allowed students twenty-four-hour access to the larger tables and no fee to play with a student ID. Her game had improved considerably since starting college. Barroom pool tables tended to be shorter so as not to take up too much drinking space. But here at the rec hall, the full-size tables were always open. Apparently, Midwest farmer-type college students weren't pool sharks. They spent more time writing term papers and reading textbooks.

Cash was learning a lot at Moorhead State College. She had already found out that most girls her age considered shooting pool a sin, against their church upbringing. While Cash drank Budweiser and wore straight-legged blue jeans and a clean T-shirt under a Levi jean jacket each day, a good handful of the students preferred smoking weed to drinking. They dressed in bell-bottom jeans and sheer peasant blouses: hippie attire. They talked about making love, not war. They flashed peace signs at each other as they crossed the green campus lawn.

And then there were the college jocks, the students from small-town, conference-winning sports teams who were big-shot scholarship jocks now. They were too undersized for any professional team they might hope to be scouted for. And who knew to look for them in the Red River Valley of the North anyway?

There were also the studious kids—students who in their small towns had been picked on, teased or ostracized because they got A's in algebra without cheating, who read *Macbeth* and enjoyed it. The ones who willingly stayed after school to create potions in the under-financed science labs of the high schools ruled by the captain of the football team and his cheerleader homecoming queen.

Cash had always played 8-ball for money, but here at college she had learned how to play 9-ball against fraternity jocks who considered it the only pool game worthy of their time. It kept her in shape for the money-making games at the Casbah—her home bar—over in Fargo, on the North Dakota side of the Red River.

She removed her cue stick from the fringe leather case she had made a few years ago. She screwed the two lengths of stick together and rolled it across the green of the nine-foot table.

She chalked the tip of her cue and broke the rack. She started with the 1-ball, then went ball by ball in numerical order, attempting a bank shot for each one into an opposite corner. She frustrated herself with her failures.

She stretched her five-foot, two-inch frame over the pool table, her cue stick resting easily on the arch made between her thumb and curled pointer finger.

"Cash, there you are!" Cash's zone was broken. *Shhh . . . t.* She nicked the edge of the cue ball sending it toward the 11 but about three inches off. She slid back off the table and turned to see Sharon hopping down the three rec hall steps, her flared bell-bottoms swirling around her platform shoes. Hippie girl.

"I was looking all over for you after science class. I'm in love! Do you think he's married? Do you think he fools around if he is? Don't you just love his hair, the way he kinda swoops it back over his forehead? And his bod . . . man."

Cash leaned over and aimed at the 11-ball again. "Who are we talking about?"

"Mr. Danielson." Sharon hopped up on the tall stool, crossed her legs and opened her long sweater jacket, her braless chest visible through the sheer gauze of her Indian-style shirt. "From now on I'm sitting in the front row, just like this." She tossed her long blond hair over her shoulder. "*You* can sit in the back row close to the door all by yourself. I want to be right up front where he can see *all* of me."

"You're crazy." Cash watched the 11-ball drop

smoothly into the far-left pocket. She scanned the table looking for the 12-ball and calculated the best angle for a bank shot. "He's an old man."

"He's only thirty."

"That's half dead."

"Mary Beth said she heard from someone that some of the teachers give A's for head."

"What the heck are you talking about?" Cash stood on tiptoe to reach across the table to line up on the 12. She was also learning that college hippie chicks wanted to talk about free love, weed and ending the war in Vietnam more than anything else.

"You know, head: a blow job, go down on him."

"There are easier ways to get an A."

"Maybe for you. Do you ever study? He is so groovy." Sharon exaggerated the flip of her hair over her other shoulder.

"Thought you had a boyfriend."

"Haven't you heard? *Make love, not war.*" Sharon giggled.

"Come on, grab a cue and play against me."

"Sure, Miss Shark. That's not a game. That's just me moving the balls around the table for you." Sharon hopped off the chair and grabbed a cue from the wall as Cash racked the balls.

Once again, Cash didn't hit the balls hard enough for any of them to drop. She was going to have to spend a few sessions just practicing her first shot, she could see.

"Open table," she said to Sharon.

Sharon walked around the table. "So . . . what should I shoot?"

"Try that solid right there. Nick the edge." Cash pointed at a spot on the purple ball. "Nick it soft and it'll drop right in."

Sharon slammed the cue ball into the solid purple. The ball dropped into the pocket followed by the cue ball. "Argghhh! This is why you ran out of class? To shoot pool?"

"Yeah, I drive shift tonight. Needed a few practice games." Cash ran five stripes before miscuing. "You have solids."

Sharon aimed at the 7-ball. "Did you hear about that chick who disappeared from Dahl Hall? Kids are saying maybe she got pregnant and went home. Then someone said she hitchhiked down to the Cities, but she hasn't come back. Her parents were at the Dean's office this morning."

Cash watched Sharon get a lucky break, accidently dropping the 7 in a side pocket.

"Nope, didn't hear that."

"That's right, you got special exemption to live off campus. I hate the dorm—curfew, no boys allowed . . ." Sharon missed her shot. "This chick was in our science class—blond, used to wear a miniskirt and sit in the front row every class? Danielson was always calling on her. She'd tilt her head and cross her legs before answering the question. His eyes were never on her face. Bet she was getting A's. Your turn."

Cash took aim at the 10. "Where's she from?"

"Who?"

"The girl who's missing, dingbat."

"Oh. Shelly?" Sharon answered as if asking Cash.

"Shelly. The town of Shelly?"

"Yeah. Why?"

"Just curious." Cash had a three-ball run and lined up to bank the fourth. She missed the shot.

"Your shot."

"Hey, Cash, you got any enemies?" Sharon asked under her breath.

"Not that I know of, why?"

Sharon rolled her eyes up toward three people—a guy and two girls—standing on the steps leading into the pool table area. They looked like they could be college students, except instead of hippie clothes they wore straight-legged jeans, T-shirts and jean jackets. Just like Cash. One of the girls had her hair in two braids that hung down the front of her jacket, the other had hers pulled back in a ponytail. The guy had messy braids, like maybe he had braided them a couple days ago and hadn't redone them yet. None of them were smiling. They were clearly looking at Cash and Sharon.

Cash lit a Marlboro. She took a long drag before she lined up on the 8-ball. Out of the corner of her eye, she saw the three of them come down the steps toward the table.

They stood watching. Finally the guy said, "Play partners? Me and her"—pointing at the girl with two braids—"against you and her."

Before Sharon got the "no" out of her mouth, Cash said, "Sure. Rack 'em up."

It was a silent game, clearly between Cash and the guy, their partners missing shots each turn. Sharon was so nervous that her cue stick shook whenever she attempted a shot. Cash played cat and mouse— not doing exactly her best but not letting him win easily either—playing just well enough to keep him convinced he was better than her but that maybe she was okay.

With one ball left and the 8-ball, he asked, "Straight 8 or last pocket?"

"Straight 8 is fine," Cash said.

His partner finally spoke. "Where you from?"

"Family's from White Earth. I live over in Fargo."

"How come we haven't seen you at any of the Indian student meetings?" asked the girl with the ponytail.

"I didn't know there were any."

"Every Friday night. At Mrs. Kills Horses."

"Potluck," said the girl with braids, missing her shot at the 8.

"Where's that?" Cash had no intention of going.

"3810 10th Avenue," the guy said. "She makes sloppy joes, so there's always something even if no one brings anything."

"And beer," said the ponytail. "If you got an ID, bring some beer."

Cash rethought going. "3810 10th Avenue?"

"Yep," said the guy, making the 8-ball and laying the cue across the table. "We're going to talk about bringing AIM up from Minneapolis."

"AIM?" It was the first time Sharon spoke since the trio had arrived.

"The American Indian Movement," answered the

girl with braids, looking the blond hippie chick up and down with a frown and one eyebrow raised.

Sharon stared back at her, peace and love gone from her blue eyes.

The girl with the braids looked at Cash and said, "See you Friday."

The three turned and left the rec hall. Cash re-racked the balls. "One more game. Then I gotta go."

"My boyfriend attended an AIM meeting down in the Cities when he was there last year for the Miig-wetch Mahnomen pow-wow. They're pretty radical. Red Power and all."

Cash wondered how Sharon knew how to pro-nounce Miigwetch and Mahnomen so perfectly, but didn't ask. Instead she said, "He goes to school over at NDSU?"

"Yeah, that's where most of the North Dakota Indians go. Something about the BIA money coming out of the Aberdeen office and NDSU being cheaper than sending them to school out of the Dakotas."

Another thing Cash hadn't known before starting college: her BIA money came out of Minneapolis because she was enrolled at the White Earth Reserva-tion, which was just about forty-five miles east from where they were standing in Moorhead, Minnesota.

When Wheaton, the county sheriff in Norman County, had convinced Cash to register for school, she learned she would be attending on a BIA scholarship. Wheaton told her the Minnesota Chippewa Tribe had signed a treaty with the United States government that guaranteed higher education to tribal members who wanted it. So she may as well go, do something with her life besides farm work, he said.

"Why don't you and your boyfriend come to the meeting on Friday night? And I can meet Mr. Free Love," said Cash, breaking the rack with force. This time the 1-ball dropped in a pocket. "I've got solids."

"Sloppy joes and beer? I'll see what he says. Can't imagine he'd turn that down. Only thing sweeter would be some good smoke," said Sharon. "He liked what those AIM folks were talking about."

"Yeah?"

"Guess they started a street patrol down in the Cities. The cops were picking up Indians from Franklin Avenue at closing time, just putting them in the trunks of their car and then dumping them down by the Mississippi or beating them up. So AIM started a patrol to get folks home safely. They talk about Indians standing up for their rights. My boyfriend says they're like the Black Panthers, but Indians."

Cash had no idea what Franklin Avenue was, but from Sharon's tone she assumed it was like NP Avenue over in Fargo where all the cheap 3.2 bars were and chronics like Ol' Man Willie started and ended the day in their favorite booth. 'Cept up here in the F-M area, it was old white men who were chronics, not Indians.

NP avenue was also where she called home, drinking at the Casbah bar each night—or each night when it wasn't beet-hauling season. She put in about an hour at the pool table after a day in the fields, playing for free drinks and the occasional dollar or five-dollar bet before heading to her apartment down the street. The only thing she knew about AIM was a couple one-night stands she'd had with a guy she called Long Braids. He had been on his way down to Minneapolis to meet up with AIM for some protest out east when their paths had crossed up Bemidji way.

"Thought those three were coming to beat you up." Sharon interrupted her thoughts, making a straight-in shot but missing her next one. "Don't know why you all look so mean all the time."

"Hmphh," breathed out Cash. She had a four-ball run before sinking the 8. She started to unscrew her cue and put it away in its fringed leather case. "Gotta get to work."

"Are you going by your apartment? Can you drop me off in Fargo?"

"Sure."

Cash and Sharon left the Student Union and headed for Cash's Ranchero. They passed groups of students on the campus lawn, studying, flirting, protesting. *Get Out of Vietnam*. Sharon talked the whole time about Danielson, then about her boyfriend's little sister who didn't like her because she was white, then again how she thought the three Indians in the pool room were coming to beat her or Cash up. Cash half-listened. With the rest of her attention, she drove and daydreamed along to Pasty Cline singing about *someone's kisses leaving her col*d.

"Can we find some rock and roll?" Sharon reached for the radio dial and changed the station. "Here we go—the Rolling Stones."

In Fargo, Cash stopped in front of the Maytag appliance store. Home. Sharon got out, waving as she walked west. Cash watched her go. She figured that after a bit Sharon would stick out her thumb to hitchhike the remaining mile to NDSU.

Cash ran up the stairs to her apartment, threw her schoolbooks and notebooks on the white enamel kitchen table that served as a place for her to study and eat. She lit a match, turned the gas burner on low under the tin coffeepot that still had coffee from the morning. She went into the next room and pulled off the clothes she had worn to school and tossed them over the overstuffed chair that held her "almost" clean clothes. She grabbed a different pair of jeans off the floor and jerked them on. It was the same pair she had been wearing all week while driving beet truck. She shook out a T-shirt and flannel shirt from the floor and put those on too.

Driving beet truck wasn't as dirty as driving during combine season when chaff and wheat bits got into all the creases of your clothes and the dust coated your hair like baby powder, but the smell of the beet plant clung to your garments. Cash figured it would be Christmas before the smell washed out completely. She wore a flannel shirt because the heater didn't always work in Milt Wang's trucks.

She quickly braided her waist-length hair into one long braid and pulled on her jean jacket. She filled her red Thermos with hot coffee and opened the fridge as if there might be food in there. Two bare shelves with a half-dozen carton of eggs looked out at her. She'd have to grab a tuna sandwich at the Silver Cup.

The evening waitress was used to Cash running

in and saying, "Tuna sandwich." The waitress, who wore her hair in a black beehive, must have seen her coming through the front window because she was already wrapping the sandwich in wax paper: tuna, mayonnaise and a leaf of lettuce between two slices of white Wonder Bread. She put her order in a small brown paper bag and folded it over neatly, just as Cash imagined all the wives of the men she worked with prepared their liverwurst or roast beef sandwiches, neatly wrapped in wax paper too, but with homemade chocolate cake or chocolate chip cookies thrown in. Some day, Cash might ask Beehive for a slice of chocolate cake to go with her tuna sandwich.

Cash put the Ranchero in reverse, then headed east to Highway 75 going north of Moorhead. Just as she was signaling to turn on 75, she changed her mind, decided to keep going straight east to the neighboring town of Hawley, where she turned north on Highway 9, a highway that would take her directly into the county seat of Ada. After a few miles she cruised through the small town of Felton, noticing several grain trucks lined up at the elevators. She drove a few miles farther, past the Lutheran Church that sat on the edge of Borup township. Still going north, she rounded a curve on the highway and crossed a bridge over the

Wild Rice River, which was not much more than a narrow creek this late in the fall.

As she came out of the curve, she saw the county sheriff's car sitting at a gravel county crossroad. She braked to a slow crawl and pulled in alongside the tan cruiser. She rolled down her window at the same time Wheaton was rolling down his. "Funding the Thanksgiving turkey giveaway?" she asked, raising an eyebrow.

"Nah, football practice is about to get over in Borup and the Ambrose boys will be speeding into Ada. One of them is dating the head cheerleader in Ada and he tries to get there just as soon as they get out of practice. One of these days he's going to come around that curve and end up in old man Peterson's field. Figure after a couple more days of seeing me sitting here, he's going to learn to slow down a bit before taking that curve. On your way to work?"

"Yeah."

"Why you coming down 9? Aren't you driving for Milt over in Halstad?"

"Yeah."

"How's school?"

"Okay."

They sat there, quiet. Cash watched the sun dip

toward the western horizon. Sheriff Wheaton watched the occasional car pass on the highway.

Cash finally spoke. "Hear anything about some girl missing from Shelly?"

"Huh? So that's why you're tracking me down."

More silence, more sky and road watching.

"Well?" asked Cash.

"You just focus on your schooling, girl. Leave the police work to me."

Cash watched the sky turn to orange, pink and purple stripes over the Red River tree line twenty-some miles west across the flat farm prairie. Almost all the fields were plowed, row after row of black dirt clods stretched for acres. To the north a corn stubble field sat unplowed, most likely being left to winter over. A green John Deere tractor, slowly pulling a plow, raised dust behind it as it traveled down a gravel road a couple of miles over.

"So where is she?" Cash finally asked. "Who is she? One of the hippie chicks at school said she's missing from our biology class."

Wheaton looked over. "You know her?"

"No. This chick just says she was in our class and now she's missing. They live in the same dorm."

"She's the oldest Tweed girl. Three younger sisters. She's in college over there to get a teaching degree."

"But she's gone."

"Yeah, I drove to Shelly Tuesday to talk to her parents after they called me. Good kid. Valedictorian. Her mom's working at the dime store in Ada to help pay her college tuition. They're heartsick. The sisters crying. Not a wild kid. Not one you'd expect to just take off and not say anything."

"Good kid, huh?"

"Why, you know something?"

"Nah, just that the hippie chick said she sits in the front of the class and flirts with the science teacher to get a good grade. Just talk. I better get to work." Cash put her arm over the back of the car seat and looked both ways down Highway 9 before backing out and heading toward Ada. In her rearview mirror, she saw Wheaton give a slight wave. She waved back before rolling up her window.

It was just on the edge of getting dark as Cash pulled into Halstad. She didn't stop in town but drove on out to Milt's farm where she exchanged her Ranchero for an International Harvester dump truck. She spent the next eight hours hauling beets back and forth from Milt's fields to the sugar beet plant just on the northern edge of Moorhead. She figured she made four trips.

Hauling beets meant driving alongside the John Deere harvester while it topped the beets, removed the green leaves, then picked them up out of the ground and carried them on a conveyor belt to the dump truck. Once the dump truck was filled, Cash drove it to the beet plant and waited in a long line with other trucks. The trucks were weighed and the farmer's name collected, assuring that the farmer would get paid the correct amount for his crop.

Some of the drivers sat in their trucks and read the daily newspaper. Others catnapped. Cash often used the time to read her homework assignments. Tonight, her curiosity was on the Valley gossip. After her first truck was weighed, she climbed out of it and walked to where a group of other drivers were standing around shooting the bull.

"Hey, Cash, thought you were too good for us already. Too busy stud-y-ing to hang out with those of us still got shit on our shoes."

Cash laughed. "Nah. Never too good for you, Bruce." Throughout junior high and high school, she and Bruce had been regulars in the wheat fields or corn furrows drinking six-pack after six-pack, listening to the country music station piped in from Oklahoma. They would drink until the beer was gone, and neither was able to walk a straight line. But he always drove her back to whatever foster place she was calling home that month.

He was one of her boy friends, never a boyfriend. White farmers were okay with their sons drinking with an Indian girl, but dating was off limits. She had learned from Bruce that his father beat his mother—"not that much really"—but Bruce had hoped to enlist and head to Vietnam as soon as he turned eighteen to get away from home. No one ever really seemed to leave the Valley. Sure, they might move to Moorhead or Crookston and get a job inside the sugar beet factory. Or maybe sell shoes at some shop on another small-town Main Street. But really, none of them ever left. They soon found themselves back plowing fields and driving beet truck for their dads or uncles, waiting for one or the other to die so they could take over the family farm.

For Bruce, some 4F reason kept him out of 'Nam. So here he was, standing in the chilly October air, smoking Salem cigarettes and bullshitting about who was going to win the World Series, who was knocked up and had to get married, and how that would never happen to him, followed by loud guffaws and back slaps. Soon the conversation would drift back to farming and the best fertilizer to put on the ground in the spring.

The guys were so used to Cash, who had been working with them in various farm labor jobs since she was eleven, that they didn't change their talk around her.

"Give me a cigarette, I left mine in the truck." Cash reached out a hand to Bruce. She lit up and took a deep drag and coughed. Bruce slapped her on the back. "Don't choke."

"Damn, forgot you smoke these menthols." Cash coughed but took another smaller drag anyway.

"You're going to school up in Moorhead?" Steve Boyer asked her.

"Yeah."

"Know anything about that Tweed girl that disappeared?"

"First I heard about it was today."

The men all jumped in, a chorus of baritones.

"Her folks are really worried."

"Valedictorian of her senior class."

"Remember when Connie Bakkas ran off with that carnie one year after the county fair and her dad had to go down to some place in Kansas to drag her back?"

"Knocked up."

"But this is Janet. That girl is smart."

"Got some legs on her too."

"Wahooo!"

"You wish."

Some more backslapping, puffs of cigarettes. Sips of coffee from foam cups that American Crystal had provided in the warm-up shack. But Cash could tell from the looks on their faces that they were worried. Bad things that happened in the Valley were the occasional fight, sometimes a car rollover from kids drag racing down a deserted road, someone got someone pregnant and had to get married. But a town's top student didn't just disappear.

"So what happened?" Cash asked.

Bruce answered. "I don't know. Folks say she was going to the Cities for the weekend with a friend from school—go see the big city and all. But her family doesn't know who she was going with or if she went or came back."

One of the other guys jumped in. "Last they heard from her was on Friday when she called home and said she was going and would call them on Sunday when she got back. She never called."

"They got phones in the Cities—I know that," another guy added.

"Let's go, trucks are moving."

They dumped the coffee cups and ground their

cigarettes out in the gravel. A roar of truck engines filled the night air as the engines turned over all at once. Gears were shifted into first to move the trucks a couple spaces forward. The trucks that had been weighed were in line to dump their beets on another conveyor belt that would move them to an ever-larger pile of beets waiting to be moved once again into the processing plant.

Cash dumped her truckload after another half hour and then returned to Milt's field, where she waited in line for another load and another trip back to Moorhead. And so the night went. She read her English assignment and decided she would talk with Mrs. Kills Horses about testing out of English, which she had overheard from some of the other students was possible. There had been one summer in the fields where she read the entire works of Shakespeare, two whole years before anyone else in her grade level ever heard of the guy. Diagramming sentences and reworking dangling participles had been an evening pastime in various foster homes where punishment often meant long hours isolated in a bedroom. This freshman English class was not only deadly boring, but it was also an early morning class. If she was able to test out of it, it would give her a couple more hours of free time.

She read her psych assignment, all about Freud being the father of modern psychology. When she finished her biology reading right around her midnight run into Moorhead, her mind went back to the Tweed girl. As Cash munched on her tuna sandwich, she closed her eyes and scanned her memory, searching for the girl in class. Cash always sat in the back row in every class, on whichever side of the room was closest to the door. Some of the students always sat in front. Whenever a teacher asked a question, they were the first to raise their hands. From the back of the room it was a sea of blondes. Scandinavian stock clearly dominated the educational system.

Last Thursday Cash had gotten to class early because Sharon wanted to copy the work Cash had done the night before. They sat at the back of the room. While Sharon cribbed her homework, Cash watched the other students file in, some in groups of three, some alone. The jocks with slicked-back hair and the hippies with scraggly, oily locks lying on their shoulders. Girls came in bell-bottoms or miniskirts.

Cash had uncanny recall ability. She could pull up a page in her science book in her mind's eye and re-read it from memory. Likewise she could pull up a day or an event and run it across a screen in her mind as if it were happening in present time. Which is what Cash did now. In her mind, Cash watched the students from last Thursday enter the room. *Ah, there she was*, the girl who must be the Tweed girl. A tall blonde—not Twiggy model thin but well-fed farmer thin—walked into the room wearing a plaid miniskirt and a mohair sweater, a book bag slung across her shoulder. She sat in the front row, front and center. Put her bag under the chair and books on the desk. Still, with her eyes almost shut, Cash scanned the room. Nothing else to see. Sun outside the window. More students coming in. Sharon closing her notebook with a sigh of relief. Mr. Danielson came into the classroom and class started. Nothing out of the ordinary.

Now Cash knew who folks were talking about when they said *the Tweed girl*.

Cash heard the other beet truck engines around her roar to life. Stretching her short frame, she pushed in the clutch with her left foot, right foot on the brake and turned the key in the ignition. She kept the truck in first as she let it roll forward to fill the space left by the other trucks. The air smelled of river mud and sugar beets mashed under truck tires. One would think it would be a syrupy, sugary smell, but it was more like stale cabbage. This fall smell was nothing compared to the rotten egg smell that would permeate the Valley come spring when the beets, which are mostly water, unfroze and the resultant fermented water filled the runoff storage ponds at the beet plant.

Cash was done hauling by two in the morning. She fetched her Ranchero from Milt's graveled farmyard, lit only by a halogen yard light, hollered See ya, followed by the obligatory hand wave to the other drivers. She sped back to Fargo, where she ran a quick bath, smoked a couple of Marlboros and drank a Bud before collapsing in bed.

When she woke in the morning, she made coffee and a fried egg sandwich, which she ate on her drive to school. It took a few turns around blocks near the campus before she found a free parking spot. She grabbed her books off the seat and walked to Mrs. Kills Horses' office in the administration building.

Mrs. Kills Horses was talking on the phone, her long black braids hanging over her full breasts. Dangly turquoise earrings matched her squash blossom necklace. She waved Cash in with a hand wearing three turquoise and silver rings. "Gotta get to work," she said into the receiver before putting the handset back in the cradle. "Good morning, Renee, how are you?" Cash could see that she was dressed in a long denim skirt. With the turquoise and braids, it made Mrs. Kills Horses look all Southwestern-y.

"Good. I was wondering what I have to do to test out of my English class?"

"Only the very best students do that, Cash."

"I'm getting all A's."

"It's kinda late in the quarter to think about that."

"Well, I'm kinda thinking about it. Maybe if you just tell me who I need to talk to?"

"You would have to do it this week or it really will be too late in the quarter."

Mrs. Kills Horses leaned over her desk and made a show of shuffling papers. When Cash didn't leave, she picked up a school catalog and made a show of flipping through the pages. Cash sat in a chair and waited. "Ah, here. Professor LeRoy is chair of the English Department."

As if you didn't know.

"You would need to talk with him about testing out. His office is in Weld Hall. You should really think about this, though," she said, looking motherly at Cash. "I can call over to the department and check on your grades if you want."

Cash, who rarely smiled, smiled. If Mrs. Kills Horses had been the observant type she would have noticed the smile didn't reach Cash's eyes— another skill she was learning at college. Cash lied, "Nah, that's okay. I'll talk with my dad about it tonight." She stood up and turned to leave the office.

"Tezhi said you were going to come to the meeting on Friday night. You'll get to meet the rest of the Indian students."

"Tezhi?"

"He said he ran into you shooting pool in the rec center?"

"Oh, yeah, Tezhi."

"It's potluck. All the Indian students come. I always make sloppy joes."

"Yeah, that's what Tezhi said," Cash said, rolling the new name off her tongue.

"We're going to plan a powwow and symposium, try to bring AIM in to discuss the rights of Indian students here on campus."

"I'll see. I might have to work."

"Work? Where are you working? You know, any job has to be reported and that could affect your BIA grant monies."

Damn, thought Cash. Seemed like there was more stuff to learn about *going* to school than there was actual course work. Thank god most farmers had no problem paying cash to their workers. Looking Mrs. Kills Horses straight in the eye, she said, "My aunt might want me to babysit. Would I have to report that?"

"Gracious, no," exclaimed Mrs. Kills Horses, her long earrings swinging with her side-to-side headshake. "Just if you are working a job, you know, like waitressing or something."

"I wouldn't know how to do that," Cash said. She was already out the door.

"See you Friday! Six-thirty," Mrs. Kills Horses called after her.

Cash walked quickly out of the administration building and took a big gulp of fall air. Being in the brick school buildings, sitting in the classrooms, even those with large windows where she could watch the clouds move across the sky, left Cash short of breath, edgy. She took another deep breath before heading resolutely across campus to Weld Hall.

Cash paused before knocking at the oak door of Professor LeRoy. She didn't know what to say to most of the people here on campus. They talked a lot, mostly about nothing. She was used to men who knew what kind of fertilizer to put on a corn field or whose main conversation was about when to spread manure on the plowed fields. And, always, the price of grain on the Minneapolis Grain Exchange. The men she knew spent little time talking and a lot of time working. The men here on campus, their work was to talk about books, authors, ideas. But rather than talk about the day's assigned reading material, class discussions often veered off into anti-war discussions or debates about civil rights. Cash wasn't sure what either of them had to do with her.

Just as she raised her fist to knock on the door, a short bearded man wearing tortoise-shell glasses opened it. Cash stepped back.

"Oh, I didn't mean to scare you," Professor LeRoy said, speaking with a rapid cadence, with an accent Cash had never heard before. "Come in, come in. I saw the shadow of your feet under the door. That's how I knew you were there. I don't have you in a class. Are you a freshman? Take a seat. What can I help you with?"

Without giving Cash a chance to answer, Professor LeRoy plowed on. "Great weather we're having, isn't it? When I moved here from New York everyone told me to appreciate the fall, that the winters would be real kickers. They weren't kidding. Just a matter of time before the snow falls, right? So what can I do for you?

You want to drop your class? Switch teachers? In my experience, one teacher is as good as the next, present company exempted. Ha." He took a breath while shuffling papers on his desk from one pile to another.

In that space Cash blurted out, "I want to test out of English 101."

Professor LeRoy stopped shuffling papers mid-air and stared at her.

"I'm a straight-A student."

"College is a little different than high school. I've been teaching here for fifteen years, and the English teachers at these farm schools have barely heard of Shakespeare, let alone Tennessee Williams or Truman Capote. Even with straight A's, I don't know how you can expect to pass a college-level test without taking the course."

"I can do it."

"Who is your teacher this quarter?"

"Mr. Horace."

"You don't like him? Other students love having him. He grades on the curve. Makes it easy to pass. You don't want to get up that early, is that it?"

"I was told students had the option to test out if they wanted. I want to test out."

LeRoy shuffled more papers. Cash watched him

silently. She wondered to herself what it was about her request that was driving Mrs. Kills Horses and now Professor LeRoy crazy.

"Most of the students who make this request were the top of their high school classes."

More silence. More shuffling of papers.

Cash lit up a Marlboro. LeRoy pushed a green glass ashtray across his desk. Smoke filled the air. Some of the anxiety left Cash's chest with each inhale.

"You're a freshman?"

"Yes. Do I have to fill out some papers or something to take the test?"

"Well." He moved more papers around, pulled a drawer open and brought more papers out. "This is the form to request the test."

Cash reached for the paper. Dean LeRoy put it down on his desk. "You sure you want to do this?"

"What happens if I fail it?" Cash asked.

"You would have to continue in Mr. Horace's class. Did you talk to him about this? Does he know you want to test out?"

"No. I talked to Mrs. Kills Horses. She gave me your name and sent me over here."

"Well, I don't know that it's such a good idea, but if you have your mind set on it, I suppose you can give it a try. You can fill out the form and then schedule a time to take the test. You would have to sit in my classroom and take it. Take it under observation."

"Today?"

"No, no, no. Fill out the form, sleep on it. Come back tomorrow and let me know if you still want to do it."

Cash put out her cigarette and reached across his desk for the form. She picked a pen up off his desk and began to fill it out. LeRoy stood up and opened the window to let some of the smoke out. He sat back down and shuffled more papers. Cash pushed the filled-out form toward him. "I'll stop back tomorrow for you to tell me what day I can take the test." She turned and almost ran out of the building, taking big gulps of air.

She walked at a fast clip all the way to her Ranchero three blocks away. She jumped in, turned the key in the ignition and drove away, straight to the Casbah, her home away from home. She used the cigarette lighter to light up.

It was too early in the day for the brothers, Ole and Carl, to be there. None of the other regulars were there either, except ol' man Willie.

Cash realized she had never been at the bar in the

morning. She usually arrived later in the evening when Willie, more often than not, was passed out in the farthest back oak booth. This early in the morning, he was sitting up at the bar, hunched over a glass of 3.2 tap beer. He looked at Cash, tipped his glass at her and said, "Oh, what is the world coming to when the young ones show up for breakfast?" He took a big gulp.

Shorty Nelson, owner and bartender, stood behind the bar, a white towel slung over his shoulder. His shirt actually looked ironed. He looked neat and put together. Not how he normally looked at the end of the night. "What are you doing here? Aren't you s'posed to be in school?"

"Give me a Bud." Cash pushed money across the polished counter. "Those folks drive me crazy."

"You drive me crazy," Willie slurred, wrapping a gray-haired arm around Cash's waist and pulling her against his side. The smell of stale armpits mixed with morning-after beer almost made Cash gag as she pushed away and jerked out of his grasp.

"Creep!"

Willie rubbed his thigh, close to his crotch, with the hand that wasn't holding his beer glass. He grinned, yellow tobacco-stained teeth appeared beneath his

Hitler-style mustache. For a split second Cash wondered how, in his constantly drunken state, he managed to maintain the perfect square above his upper lip, but then an involuntary shudder shook her body as she noticed the bulge in his pants, the pants still stained from last night's drunk.

"Jeezus," she said, grabbing the Bud, taking a big drink and heading to the coin-operated pool table. She dug four quarters out of her jeans pocket, put them in the coin slot and listened to the comforting sound of billiard balls dropping. She grabbed a house cue because she hadn't even thought to bring her own, rolled it across the green felt, saw that it was warped a bit, put that one back and took another. That one was a bit straighter, if a tad lighter, but it would work. She racked the balls and in one fluid movement removed the wooden triangle, seized the cue stick, leaned over the table and sent the cue ball flying into the racked balls, causing three of them to drop into separate pockets.

Shorty leaned on his forearms across the bar, watching Cash play against herself. "You know, Cash, Willie here used to be one of the richest farmers in the Valley."

"Still am," interrupted Willie.

"Until he took to coming in here mornings. Soon he was spending more time drinking than plowing."

"I can still plow." Willie leered for Shorty's benefit, rubbing his thigh again, tipping his glass in Cash's direction before killing it off. He wiped the beer foam from his mustache with his forearm and pointed the glass at Shorty. "Another. That's why I had sons. They run the farm for me since my arthritis kicked in. They don't need a college degree to farm."

Shorty refilled his glass saying, "Just shut up and drink, old man. Cash, you got a good thing going, kid. What are you doing here instead of at class?"

Cash leaned on her cue stick. She stared hard at Shorty, willing him to shut up.

"Don't you know Ole and Carl are in here every night bragging to anyone who will listen about how you are going to college? Everyone's proud of you."

"Damn straight," said Willie, lifting his refilled glass.

"Shut up," Cash said under her breath, sending the 9-ball into a side pocket. To Shorty, she said, "I just don't know, Shorty. It's a whole different world."

"You're smart, Cash."

"I don't think smart is the issue," said Cash, lining up the cue ball on the 2-ball, sitting three inches off a corner pocket. "These folks talk a different language. Dress different. Sit inside brick buildings all day and think of fancy ways to string words together instead of just saying things plain out. Plus, I think the teachers all think I'm stupid just because I'm Indian. I'm not used to folks treating me like I'm stupid. Being mean or calling me names or being disgusting," she said, pointing her cue stick toward Willie, "that, I'm used to, but being thought of as stupid just because I'm Indian? Pisses me off." She dropped the 8-ball into the same corner as the 2. With the table cleared, she put four more quarters into the table and racked the balls.

As she broke and started shooting, she said, "And these beginner classes are dumb. I learned all this stuff in high school. I don't see why I have to take it all over again. I heard that students can test out of these baby classes, but when I asked, everyone treated me like I'm just a dumb Indian."

"Are they gonna let you though?" asked Shorty, flicking his rag across the counter again.

Cash stood up from the table and looked at him across the bar. She took a drink of her Bud and a drag of her cigarette. "I filled out the *form* to test out of English this morning," she said with heavy sarcasm. "I'm going to go talk to the chair again tomorrow to find out when he'll let me take the test." She shot a couple more balls into the table before continuing.

"Then I'll go talk to the chair of the science department about trying to test out of his class too. I can already recite the periodic table frontwards and backwards. I know photosynthesis is what makes us rich here in the Bread Basket of the World." Cash waved her cue stick and beer bottle in a wide arc. "I don't think I need to be in a classroom, getting a sore ass sitting on hard chairs, smelling some strange oil these hippies wear to cover the smell of the marijuana they smoke, just to have some old guy tell me that corn and sugar beets need sun to grow." Cash started furiously shooting balls into pockets. "If I test out, I can just take my psychology and judo classes. Classes I might actually learn something in."

"Can you do that? I mean, do they let students just test out of classes?" Shorty asked.

"That's what it says in the student handbook," answered Cash. "If I can test out, I'll be free for the rest of the quarter." She swung her cue over the pool table. "And I can get my game back. I don't think I was cut out to sit inside brick buildings."

"You're still driving truck at night, right?"

"Yeah, that's why I haven't been in to shoot. School

all day, driving truck at night. I just couldn't take it anymore this morning. At school, they have these big 9-foot tables. I go over there and play between classes, but I miss this," she said, waving her cue around the bar, taking another drink of beer and a drag of her Marlboro. "Did you hear about that girl from the college who is missing?"

Shorty wiped the bar with his rag, sopping up the beer Willie had spilled while pushing himself off the bar stool for an unsteady walk to the bathroom. At least he was making it there, not using the back booth, as was his nightly habit. All the regulars knew never to sit in that booth and newcomers soon moved because of the stench.

"Some of the folks were talking. Then there was an article in *The Forum*."

"Oh? I didn't see that."

"Yeah, just how she seems to have gone to the Cities and hasn't been heard from since. Her folks are all worried."

"She's in my science class. Was."

"Whaddya think happened?"

"I don't know. I talked to Wheaton last night. He's asking around." Cash cleared the table of all the billiard balls. "I s'pose I better go back." She returned the bar cue to an empty slot on the wall rack. "Guess I've missed my English class, but I can still make science, then this afternoon my last class is judo. Soon I'll be able to kick fools off bar stools." She pantomimed a sidekick in Willie's direction.

"Keep your nose in the books," Shorty hollered as the bar door closed behind her.

Other Titles in the Soho Crime Series

SEICHŌ MATSUMOTO
(Japan)
Inspector Imanishi Investigates

MAGDALEN NABB
(Italy)
Death of an Englishman
Death of a Dutchman
Death in Springtime
Death in Autumn
The Marshal and the Murderer
The Marshal and the Madwoman
The Marshal's Own Case
The Marshal Makes His Report
The Marshal at the Villa Torrini
Property of Blood
Some Bitter Taste
The Innocent
Vita Nuova
The Monster of Florence

FUMINORI NAKAMURA
(Japan)
The Thief
Evil and the Mask
Last Winter, We Parted
The Kingdom
The Boy in the Earth
Cult X
My Annihilation

STUART NEVILLE
(Northern Ireland)
The Ghosts of Belfast
Collusion
Stolen Souls
The Final Silence
Those We Left Behind
So Say the Fallen
The Traveller & Other Stories
House of Ashes

(Dublin)
Ratlines

KWEI QUARTEY
(Ghana)
Murder at Cape Three Points
Gold of Our Fathers
Death by His Grace

KWEI QUARTEY CONT.
The Missing American
Sleep Well, My Lady

QIU XIAOLONG
(China)
Death of a Red Heroine
A Loyal Character Dancer
When Red Is Black

MARCIE R. RENDON
(Minnesota's Red River Valley)
Murder on the Red River
Girl Gone Missing

JAMES SALLIS
(New Orleans)
The Long-Legged Fly
Moth
Black Hornet
Eye of the Cricket
Bluebottle
Ghost of a Flea

Sarah Jane

JOHN STRALEY
(Sitka, Alaska)
The Woman Who Married a Bear
The Curious Eat Themselves
The Music of What Happens
Death and the Language
  of Happiness
The Angels Will Not Care
Cold Water Burning
Baby's First Felony
So Far and Good

(Cold Storage, Alaska)
The Big Both Ways
Cold Storage, Alaska
What Is Time to a Pig?

AKIMITSU TAKAGI
(Japan)
The Tattoo Murder Case
Honeymoon to Nowhere
The Informer

CAMILLA TRINCHIERI
(Tuscany)
Murder in Chianti
The Bitter Taste of Murder

HELENE TURSTEN
(Sweden)
Detective Inspector Huss
The Torso
The Glass Devil
Night Rounds
The Golden Calf
The Fire Dance
The Beige Man
The Treacherous Net
Who Watcheth
Protected by the Shadows

Hunting Game
Winter Grave
Snowdrift

An Elderly Lady Is Up
  to No Good
An Elderly Lady Must Not
  Be Crossed

ILARIA TUTI
(Italy)
Flowers over the Inferno
The Sleeping Nymph

JANWILLEM VAN DE WETERING
(Holland)
Outsider in Amsterdam
Tumbleweed
The Corpse on the Dike
Death of a Hawker
The Japanese Corpse
The Blond Baboon
The Maine Massacre
The Mind-Murders
The Streetbird
The Rattle-Rat
Hard Rain
Just a Corpse at Twilight
Hollow-Eyed Angel
The Perfidious Parrot
The Sergeant's Cat:
  Collected Stories

JACQUELINE WINSPEAR
(1920s England)
Maisie Dobbs
Birds of a Feather